Christina was aware of his nearness

She hugged herself nervously, but ventured, "But it hasn't been forgotten, has it? You constantly defend your appearance when no defense is necessary."

"You think not?" he bit out violently, taking her by the shoulders and swinging her roughly around to face him. "Could you bear to kiss me, Christina? Could you bear to press those soft cheeks against my face?"

His hands were stopping her struggles, then he dragged her close against the hard length of his body, pressing his face—his scarred face—against hers.

It was ecstasy to be this close to him, to feel the heavy pounding of his heart beneath her fingers, to know that for once she had broken down the barriers he had erected between himself and the rest of humanity.

1 Master of Falcon's Head (Presents #69)

2 The Japanese Screen (Presents #77)

3 Rachel Trevellyan (Presents #86)

4 Mask of Scars (Presents #92)

5 Dark Moonless Night (Presents #100)

6 Witchstone (Presents #110)

ANNE MATHER

Mask of Scars

Harlequin Books

TORONTO • NEW YORK • LOS ANGELES • LONDON
AMSTERDAM • PARIS • SYDNEY • HAMBURG
STOCKHOLM • ATHENS • TOKYO • MILAN

First Harlequin edition published May 1975

ISBN 0-373-10092-2

This *Harlequin Salutes* edition published February 1983

Original hardcover edition published in 1973
by Mills & Boon Limited

CHAPTER ONE

By the time the train pulled into the station at Lagos, Christina felt she had had a surfeit of glorious country-side and even more delightful coastline lit by the brilliance of the Mediterranean sun, and she would have been prepared to forgo such beauty in favour of a cooling shower and a change of clothes. Although she was wearing the minimum in underwear, the thin cotton jeans were clinging to her slender legs and the pink shirt which had been crisp and attractive when she set out from the *pensao* in Lisbon that morning was now limp, too. She felt hot and sticky and she half wished she had buried her pride and used the money Bruce had sent to buy an air ticket to Portugal.

But knowing her sister-in-law as she did she was firmly convinced that she knew nothing of her husband's generosity, and it was quite within Sheila's capabilities for her to question how Christina, who was apparently without funds, could afford the air fare to Faro. And the very last thing Christina wanted was to create friction between her brother and his wife at the start of her stay.

Lagos was the train terminal and there were several other passengers disembarking as Christina tugged her duffel bag and rather shabby suitcase on to the platform. Some of the other passengers were tourists, and in expensive continental gear and with porters carrying their blatantly new suitcases they were in complete contrast to Christina's crumpled appearance. But she didn't mind. With the inconsequence of youth it never troubled her what anyone thought about her, and she tossed back the curtain of corn-coloured hair that fell straightly about her shoulders as she bent to lift the duffel bag on to her back, and regarded her fellow passengers with something like amused tolerance in her clear grey eyes.

Outside the station the taxis were quickly commandeered and Christina looked about her doubtfully, wondering which way was the bus station. If she had troubled to inform Bruce of her estimated time of arrival, she knew he would have either sent someone to meet her or come himself, but she preferred the independence of making her own arrangements, a trait which had landed her in trouble at the University on more than one occasion.

Lagos seemed an attractive little town and even at this early hour of the evening, there were plenty of people strolling about, enjoying the sunshine or taking coffee at one or other of the exotic little open-air cafés and restaurants. Christina would have liked to have had some coffee and a sandwich herself, but Bruce's small hotel was not here, it was at Porto Cedro, and she realised she would have to make some definite move towards getting there before it was dark.

Dropping her suitcase, she rummaged in her duffel bag and brought out a rather tattered-looking map which she had picked up for a few pence in Chelsea High Street, and spreading it awkwardly, she traced the line of her route from Lagos to the small village where her brother lived. According to the map it was some five miles west on the road to Sagres, and with an indifferent shrug she folded the map again and put it away. Five miles wasn't far. She could probably walk it more easily than she could struggle to find the bus station when her knowledge of Portuguese was limited to a phrase book tucked into her jeans' pocket.

Swinging the duffel bag back on to her shoulders,

6

she made her way towards the outskirts of the small town, using the coastline as a guide. But as she neared the steep cliffs which fell away to a beach bleached almost white by the sun she wanted to linger and savour the knowledge that for three months she would be able to feast her eyes on such scenes and luxuriate in the deepening warmth of the sun. She longed to go down on the beach and find coolness in the creaming blue waters that lapped the shoreline, but common sense told her that she could not do so now. But tomorrow, she promised herself fiercely, tomorrow...

The road to Sagres was dusty and narrow, and although the sun was sinking it was still very hot. Christina ran a hand round the back of her neck under the weight of her hair and sighed in incredulity when she considered that it had been raining when she left London yesterday and for June the weather was unseasonably cold. Or was it? she thought wryly. Wasn't English weather always unseasonable?

A lumbering cattle truck passed her, throwing up a cloud of dust which made her stop and cough chokingly for a moment. The driver halted and waved to her, obviously offering a lift, but although the prospect was inviting Christina declined. It wasn't that she had never accepted a lift before, but simply that she preferred to take this slower pace. After all, no matter how attractive these three months in Porto Cedro might seem, she was quite aware that Sheila would demand and get value for her so-called hospitality, and Christina was prepared to make beds and scrub floors and wash dishes and do all the mundane tasks necessary to the efficient upkeep of a small hotel. But no matter how arduous these three months might be, at the end of each day she would be her own mistress, and there was always Bruce to share her enjoyment with.

She trudged on, the suitcase getting heavier by the

minute and the duffel bag's ropes digging into her shoulders. She should have taken the lift she had been offered. She would have been in Porto Cedro by now. She sighed. The last signpost a few yards back had said only four more kilometres to the village. Surely they would not take her much longer now.

A couple of cars passed her going in the opposite direction and she thought how wonderful it would be if she were to meet Bruce in that way. But then perhaps not, she amended to herself dryly. If Sheila were with him she would be horrified at Christina choosing to walk all this way along roads she did not know when anyone might happen along to molest her. But then Sheila was a very correct person, and perhaps that was why she and Christina had never got along very well together. It was not that Christina was entirely irresponsible; it was simply that Sheila did not and had not ever understood the independence of youth.

The sound of tyres on the dusty road came to Christina's ears and she glanced round in time to see a huge black limousine approaching. With a casual movement she jerked her thumb in the direction she was going, her thoughts of Sheila goading her into doing the very thing she knew her sister-in-law would most disapprove of.

But she need not have bothered. The huge car with its sleek lines and a rather curious insignia engraved on its side swept past in complete indifference to her presence, although as the dust surged over her Christina was indignantly aware that the car had passed deliberately closely, almost forcing her on to the grass verge.

Hunching her shoulders, Christina looked resentfully after the retreating chauffeur-driven vehicle and then with a characteristic shrug, she again pressed on.

At last the outlying cottages of the village came into view and Christina could not suppress the wave of excitement that enveloped her. It was almost a year since she had last seen her brother and previously they had been very close, not even Sheila's jealous hostility causing more than a brief ripple on the surface of their friendship.

In his letter Bruce had told her that the Hotel Inglês stood above a small cove. He had said that the whole area was riddled with small coves and rocky promontories giving way to caves and rock-pools when the tide was out. He had said the swimming was excellent and that he himself had taken up snorkelling and skin-diving. He had said the sea was amazingly clear, and looking down on its lucid depths Christina could quite believe it.

Porto Cedro nestled on the side of the cliffs, a market square providing a small bus station and its focal point a stone fountain. The houses around the square were painted in pastel shades with white shutters and deliciously hanging eaves that provided slanting patches of shade on the paths. Some had grilles in wrought iron, and arches, relics of Moorish occupation and influence. There was something faintly eastern about it and Christina found it all very picturesque. Her vivid imagination conjured up scenes of Moorish pirates swarming along these narrow streets swinging cutlasses and carrying off the most beautiful women for their harems.

She smiled to herself suddenly and in so doing attracted the attention of a group of young men passing by so that they spoke to her invitingly in their own language, raising their dark eyebrows and allowing their breath to be expelled in low whistles.

Christina shook her head almost imperceptibly and turned determinedly through a walk between tall dark houses that led to the sea-front. to her relief she saw the sign for the Hotel Inglês almost immediately. Porto Cedro did not sport many hotels, and in fact the Hotel Inglês was little more than a glorified *pensao*. In the glittering rays of the setting sun, it looked less glamorous somehow than she had imagined it, some of the paintwork peeling in the heat, the tables standing carelessly before it still covered in dirty crockery where someone, tourists possibly, had taken afternoon tea. But for all that she felt a surge of pride that Bruce should have such an establishment, and she walked quickly up the shallow steps and through the screen of hanging plastic beads that protected the hall from the glare of the sun.

The hall was tiled in plastic tiles and there was a small reception desk on which was a bell which indicated its use for attention. But Christina hesitated a moment before pressing it. She wanted to look around and absorb her surroundings before she warned anyone of her arrival.

From the hall, arched doorways led into the dining room and another room which could have been a lounge. To the left was the small bar, deserted at the moment, without even a barman to attend to any customer who might suddenly appear. Everywhere was clean, spotlessly so, and Christina's spirits rose. It was foolish to allow this ominous feeling of anti-climax to cloud her happiness at being here—with Bruce.

The sound of footsteps coming along the corridor to her right caused her to swing round sharply just as Sheila, her sister-in-law, was beginning: '*Sinto muito, menina*——' But she broke off in obvious astonishment as she recognised Christina and her face changed remarkably from smiling welcome to veiled hostility: '*Christina!* In heaven's name, Christina, what are you doing here?'

Christina felt the first twinges of real anxiety. 'I—I walked here—from the station at Lagos!'

Sheila shook her head incredulously. 'But what are you doing here in Portugal? I thought you were at university!'

Christina's fingers fumbled with the ropes of her duffel bag. 'I was. It's the summer vac, Sheila.'

Sheila Ashley spread a hand helplessly. 'Christina, maybe I'm phrasing my questions badly, or maybe you're deliberately misunderstanding me, I don't know, but I want to know why, even if it is the summer vacation, you're here!'

Christina's anxieties crystallised into real doubts. 'Do—do you mean to say—I'm not expected?' she ventured carefully, her grey eyes never leaving her sister-in-law's face.

Sheila Ashley was an attractive woman. In her early thirties she had all the poise and elegance of a fashion model. Tall and slim, with sleek dark hair knotted at the back of her head, she had none of the slightly harassed air sometimes visible in the faces of married women, and Christina privately thought that that was because nothing ever moved Sheila. Nothing ever troubled her more than slightly, and as she had no children no disfiguring bulk of pregnancy had ever marred that slender frame. But right now Sheila was disturbed. It was visible in the tightening of her lips, in the narrowing of her dark eyes, in the way she plucked almost nervously at the fine material of her thin dress.

'How could you be?' she began now, in answer to Christina's question. 'We didn't even know the term was over.'

Christina felt an overwhelming sense of impatience. It was obvious now. Bruce had not told his wife she was coming. And because she had not written to let him know when she was arriving he had not had a chance to tell her. She should have known that Sheila would be the last person to welcome her young sister-in-law into their home.

But now Christina had to say something, and realising it would serve no useful purpose to explain that

Bruce had written to her inviting her to stay and help them with the hotel, she said:

'I naturally assumed that once the university closed I would be welcome here for a couple of weeks. Now that Father's dead——'

'But you should have let us know you were coming, Christina,' Sheila burst out. 'I mean, your father's been dead ten months now, and you must have realised before the term ended that you would have to find a job of sorts to support yourself now that university's closed!'

Christina hesitated. 'Actually, I thought I might help you here, Sheila.'

Sheila's eyes widened in amazement. 'You mean— you mean work here—in the hotel!'

'Yes.' Christina glanced through the open doorway towards the uncleared tables on the forecourt. 'Don't you need some help?'

Sheila was clearly battling within herself now, unable to find any logical reason to reject such a suggestion. 'We manage,' she began. 'There's not just Bruce and me, you know. Julio serves in the bar in the evenings, and Maria does all the cooking.'

Christina wondered where Bruce could be. Standing here in the hall like this, arguing with Sheila, was hardly the welcome she had envisaged, and she had the distinct feeling that Sheila would send her away without even seeing her brother if she could.

'Where is Bruce?' she questioned now. 'Isn't he here?'

'No—yes—that is, he's out right now.' Sheila bit her lip. 'Look, Christina, I don't want to hurt your feelings, but quite honestly you're not the type to work in the hotel.' She surveyed Christina's appearance critically. 'What on earth could you do?'

'I can make beds, wash dishes—anything you like.' Christina sighed. 'Do you think I could have a cup of tea? I'm terribly thirsty.'

Sheila gave in with ill grace. Short of physically ejecting Christina from the building there was little else she could do. 'Very well,' she agreed shortly. 'Come through here. Our rooms are at the back of the hotel.'

Christina followed her sister-in-law along a white-emulsioned passage to a room at the back of the building which overlooked a walled garden. It was not a big garden, but it was a veritable wilderness of flowers and flowering shrubs. Christina stared out at the confusion in delight, wondering how anyone could allow such beauty to go to waste.

Sheila, noticing her interest, commented off-handedly: 'We don't have time to attend to the garden. When Bruce has the time, he's going to find a gardener.'

Christina thought she might have added, when Bruce can *afford* it, but she refrained from making any response and dropping her duffel bag and suitcase thankfully, she flung herself into a low basket weave chair. Sheila walked through into a small kitchen, and Christina could hear her filling the kettle and setting cups on saucers. There was a kind of suppressed violence about the way each cup clattered into its place, and Christina sighed, cupping her chin on one hand dejectedly. She had expected antipathy from Sheila, but not to this extent.

Sheila came back into the room. 'How long did you expect to stay?' she asked abruptly.

Christina was taken aback. 'Does it matter?'

'Of course it matters. Christina, this is Porto Cedro, not the Kings Road! Things are different here. Oh, I don't know how I'm going to explain this to you, but —well, your ways are so very different from ours. People here are not so—easy-going, as they are back in England. I can't speak for Portugal as a whole, of course, but here in the Algarve, in Porto Cedro par-

13

ticularly, we observe the codes of conduct that have been upheld here for centuries!'

Christina frowned. 'Don't you mean the rules for the Portuguese?'

'Yes, of course. And as we live here—we make our living in this village—we are expected to conform, too.'

'You can't be serious!' Christina stared at her.

'Of course I'm serious. That's why I find your presence here so hard to condone. Christina, you're a nice girl, and I've no doubt in England your attitudes would go unnoticed——'

'What do you mean? My attitudes?' Christina was stung by the scathing note in Sheila's voice.

'Well, honestly, dear, one doesn't wear slacks, let alone jeans, unless one is going sailing, of course. And young women are protected here. They're not even allowed to mix with their fiancés unless a chaperon is on hand——'

'But I'm not Portuguese, Sheila——'

'But can't you see, Christina, I'm trying to explain. When one lives in a country—when one makes one's living from that country—one is expected to observe the rules.'

'Rules!' Christina raised her eyes heavenward. 'Honestly, Sheila, you can't expect me to believe that no tourists appear here dressed as I'm dressed. That everyone who visits Porto Cedro observes these so-called rules!'

'Of course I'm not saying that. As a tourist I suppose you'd go unnoticed. But you're not a tourist, are you, Christina? You're Bruce's sister. And once that gets about, you'll be expected to behave as we do.'

Christina hunched her shoulders. 'Why don't you just say you don't want me here whatever the circumstances and be done with it?' she demanded hotly. 'You don't really expect me to stomach all that rub-

14

bish about my clothes and mixing with the opposite sex—and being *protected*, do you?'

Sheila stiffened. 'All right, Christina. As you insist on putting everything in such crude terms, I'll be honest. I admit I don't want you here. But regardless of anything I feel personally, the situation remains the same. You simply wouldn't fit in.'

'What's going on here? *Christina!*'

The male voice that broke into their conversation brought both women up short. Bruce Ashley stood in the doorway, tall and broad and to Christina, dearly familiar. She flung herself out of her chair and across the room into his arms, uncaring what Sheila might think.

Bruce held her closely for a few minutes and then he held her at arm's length and stared at her as though he could not believe his eyes. 'Christina! What the hell do you mean by appearing like this? Why didn't you let me know so that I could meet you? Have you come by air?'

Christina shook her head quickly. 'Where would I get the money to buy an air ticket?' she asked meaningfully, holding his eyes with hers, trying to convey wordlessly what had passed between herself and Sheila.

Bruce frowned, but he seemed to gather what she meant, for he inclined his head slowly, and said: 'Well, anyway, you should have written and told us when to expect you.'

Sheila looked at him suspiciously. 'Did you know Christina was coming, Bruce?' she asked sharply.

Bruce hesitated. 'I thought she might. Why not? We're her only kin. Why shouldn't she come here? This is her home?'

'Christina is eighteen, Bruce. Not a child.'

'Eighteen? What's eighteen?' Bruce chewed his lip. 'If we'd still been living in Kensington, she'd have come to us then, wouldn't she?'

'Maybe. But we're not still living in Kensington, Bruce. The situation here is different—I've been trying to explain. Christina just wouldn't fit in here. She's not used to restrictions.'

'What nonsense!' Bruce released Christina and felt about in his pockets for his cigarettes. 'Why shouldn't she fit in here? She—er—she could help about in the hotel. That way she'd earn her keep.'

Sheila pushed past him and walked into the kitchen to make the tea. When she came back with the tray a few moments later Christina could see she was having difficulty controlling her temper.

Meanwhile Bruce had flung himself into a comfortable chair and was asking Christina about her work at the university. It had been unfortunate that Mr. Ashley had died within a week of her taking up her studies, but the different environment had in some ways allayed the grief she would otherwise have suffered. They had been very close, she and her father, particularly since Bruce was married and his wife had never shown any desire to involve herself with her husband's family. Christina's mother had died when she was twelve, and she remembered her only as a rather fragile individual, always suffering from headaches and ill health, spending her days on the couch in the lounge of the house they had had in Wimbledon.

The previous May, Bruce and Sheila had left England to open this hotel in Porto Cedro, and the last time Christina had seen Bruce had been when he flew home for her father's funeral. During the subsequent Christmas and Easter holidays she had found accommodation and work to support herself, but it had been Bruce's suggestion that she should come and spend the long summer vacation with them. The little money her father had left barely kept her in spending money during term time and she had been glad of the chance to see Bruce and possibly help him in whatever capa-

16

city she could. She had fondly imagined Sheila had mellowed towards her. It was only now she realised how hopeless that thought had been.

Now Sheila placed the tray on the low table before Bruce and added milk to the cups, pouring the tea with precise movements.

'Sugar?' she enquired of Christina, but Christina shook her head awkwardly.

'No, thanks.'

Sheila left her husband's tea on the tray and then went to sit in another chair. 'And where is she to sleep?' she asked, at last.

Christina stood down her cup. 'Really, Sheila, I think it would be as well if I left,' she said carefully. 'It's obvious you don't want me here, and it would be impossible for me to stay under those circumstances.'

Sheila's features relaxed slightly. 'I'm glad you see——' she was beginning, when Bruce interrupted her.

'*Sheila!*' He bit out the word angrily, and got to his feet. 'I will not allow you to speak to my sister like this! I don't give a damn what your opinion is, this is my home, too, and I'll invite who I like to it, do I make myself clear?'

Sheila froze. 'How dare you speak to me like that? Just because Christina chooses to land herself upon us——'

'She didn't choose to land herself upon us!' snapped Bruce shortly, and waved away the restraining hand Christina placed on his sleeve. 'I wrote and invited her to stay with us for the summer vacation. I also sent her enough money to cover the air fare. As she hasn't used it, I can only assume she didn't want to feel beholden to me to that extent!'

Sheila rose now. 'You sent her the money!' she exclaimed disbelievingly.

'Yes. Why not? For God's sake, Sheila, be reasonable——'

'Reasonable! *Reasonable!* When I'm slaving my fingers to the bone to make this place pay, and your blessed sister spends her days doing nothing more arduous than attending lectures and writing up a few notes in a book! She's eighteen, Bruce! In the circumstances, I think it's high time she was earning a living!'

'Oh, please——' began Christina helplessly. 'Don't go on! I'll—I'll go back to England tomorrow.'

'You will not!' Bruce turned an angry face towards her. 'Leave this to me!' He looked back at Sheila. 'Must I remind you that it was my money that leased this hotel? You haven't done a stroke of work outside our home since we got married, and if I choose to send a little of my money to my sister, then I don't think you should complain.'

Sheila's face suffused with colour. 'That's a foul thing to say!' she exclaimed, her voice less belligerent now.

'Yes. Well, don't you think what you've already said is foul, too? Making Christina feel as though she's some kind of hanger-on? I repeat—this is Christina's home for as long as she wants it to be.'

Sheila sought the refuge of her chair, putting a hand to her forehead. 'I've got the most dreadful headache now,' she said, rather faintly. 'You don't care about me at all, Bruce. Just so long as your sister doesn't suffer.'

'For God's sake, Sheila, that's not true.'

'It is true.' To Christina's horror tears of self-pity overflowed from Sheila's eyes and ran down her pale cheeks.

Bruce looked helplessly at his sister and with a sigh Christina got to her feet and left the room. She was glad to go. The atmosphere in there was so thick that you could have cut it with a knife, and she had no desire to see Bruce make a fool of himself over a few crocodile tears.

She walked outside. It was appreciably darker now, the sun sinking in a blaze of glory in the west. The hotel stood on the cliffs and to the right a steep road led down to the sea-front where lights were beginning to twinkle in the twilight. She could see a harbour and a small jetty with several fishing boats moored along its length. There was something warm and reassuring about these everyday sights and on impulse she walked down the road to the sea-front and leant on the harbour wall. She had no wish to return to the hotel yet. She still wasn't sure what she was going to do. It was all very well for Bruce to force Sheila to accept her, but what kind of life would she have with her sister-in-law picking on her every minute of the day? Could she stand it? Even for Bruce's sake?

Leaving the wall, she skirted the harbour and jumped down on to the stretch of beach beyond it. The soft sand ran between her toes and she walked slowly on, her hands thrust into the pockets of her jeans.

Ahead a wall of rock divided one cove from the other, but there was an aperture wide enough for Christina to slide through and she found herself on an isolated stretch of shoreline where the water creamed with inviting coolness.

There seemed no access to the beach, other than through the aperture she had breached, and she walked towards the sea, kicking off her sandals and allowing the water to ripple over her toes. It was a sensuous feeling. She had never bathed in warm waters before, and she wished she had had the good sense to bring her bathing suit with her. The idea of submerging her hot, sticky body in those cooling depths was almost more than she could bear.

Without stopping to consider the advisability of her

actions, Christina quickly stripped off all her clothes and ran to dive headlong into the waves. It was glorious, the water still warm from the rays of the sun, and the heat of the day melted from her body leaving her refreshed and alert.

She swam and played for fully fifteen minutes, her hair like seaweed about her in the water, before she became aware that she was no longer alone. Out on the shore, silhouetted against the darkening velvet of the sky and partially hidden by the shadow of the cliffs, stood a man, the tip of his cigarette, or cigar, visible as it was regularly raised to his lips to glow more brightly before becoming subdued again.

Christina trod water and considered her position. Her clothes lay on the beach, some distance from the intruder, it was true, but nevertheless far enough up the beach to cause her some discomfort. She sighed. Had he seen her, or was he simply out for an evening stroll? Could he be unaware that someone was swimming only a hundred yards away?

She wrinkled her nose impatiently. In half an hour, maybe less, it would be dark, but already she was beginning to feel cold, and in half an hour she would be much colder. Truthfully, until then she had not realised how cold she was, but anxiety produced its own lowering of the temperature.

To her horror, the man began to walk down the beach to the water's edge and he halted by her small pile of clothes regarding them intently. Now she could see he was a tall man, lean and dark, sideburns growing down almost to his jawline. Although the features of his face were indistinct in the fading light, she sensed an air of authority, of haughty arrogance about him, and she wondered who he could be. He did not appear like one of the villagers and she was pondering the possibility of him being a tourist when he turned his dark head in her direction. Immediately her hopes of remaining unobserved vanished.

'*Tenha a bondade de sair, menina,*' he snapped shortly. '*Vai-se fazendo tarde!*'

Christine hadn't the faintest idea what he was saying, but it seemed obvious from his attitude and the uncompromising tone of his voice that he was not at all pleased at her appearance.

Endeavouring to remember the right words from her phrase book, Christina called: '*Nao falo portugues, senhor!*'

The man threw away the butt of his cigarette and advanced to the water's edge. Now Christina could see the patrician cast of his features and the slightly cruel line of his mouth. But what caught her attention most was the long, jagged scar which ran down his left cheek, from the corner of his eye almost to his jawline. The livid whiteness of that grim disfiguration was all the more pronounced because of the swarthiness of his skin, and it gave his aquiline face an almost satanic appearance.

'So, *menina*, you are English!' he was saying coldly now, his expression revealing his awareness of her scrutiny. 'Then please to come out. This is a private beach, and you are trespassing!'

His faint accent was attractive, and so was his voice, but what he was saying was not. There was a contemptuous twist to his lips and he was regarding her as though she was some particularly obnoxious specimen washed up on his beach. To be charitable she supposed his disfiguration might account for a little of his bitterness, but to Christina it was nothing to be ashamed of. Indeed, if anything it gave strength and character to a face which might otherwise have been merely handsome in an aristocratic, Latin way.

'My clothes are behind you, *senhor!*' she said now, glad of the concealing depths of the water as his cold gaze raked her. 'If you'll go away I'll do exactly as you ask.'

The man's curiously light eyes narrowed. 'You are trespassing, *menina*, as I have said. I prefer to stay and escort you off my property myself.'

Christina sighed, wrinkling her nose. 'As you wish, *senhor*. But at least have the goodness to turn the other way.'

He frowned. 'You mean——' He stared at her incredulously. '*Dues nao permita! Tu adolescentes!*' The narrow fingers clenched. '*Esta bem, menina,* I will walk towards the cliffs. But you will not disappear in my absence!'

Christina did not reply, and he hesitated a moment. 'Wait! I have seen you before, *menina*, have I not? You were—how do you say it—hitching—is that right? *Sim*, hitching a lift earlier this evening on the road from Lagos, were you not?'

Christina nodded, and then her eyes widened. 'You were in the limousine?'

'Where I was is not important, *menina*. What concerns me is where you intended to sleep tonight. On my beach, perhaps?'

'Of course not!' Christina was stung by his accusation.

'Why—of course not?' The man's lip curled. 'Believe me, *menina*, we have had trouble with young people like yourself before. What is it you call yourselves? Freedom-lovers—is that right? We have other names for what you do!'

'How charming!' Christina refused to show the outrage she felt at the disparaging way he was dismissing her. It was not often anyone got under her skin, but this man did. 'I'm cold, *senhor*,' she went on indolently. 'Unless you want me to put on my clothes under your malevolent gaze, go away!'

The man's nostrils flared, and Christina thought

almost detachedly that he was a most disturbingly masculine animal. Despite the formal attire, the expensive silk grey suit, the fine shirt, and grey tie, the soft suede boots on his feet, there was an air of indomitability about him, of ruthless overbearing strength, that no amount of civilisation could entirely subdue. She wondered what mixture of blood ran in his veins that he could at once appear cool and clinical, hard and passionate. And that scar, that unholy blemish, added the final touch to a cruel, and possibly violent, nature.

Without another word he turned and walked away up the beach and Christina hastened out of the water, shivering quite forcefully now. She put her clothes on to her wet skin, allowing them to dry her, and wrung out her hair carelessly. As her body grew warmer she realised that her trembling was due as much to nerves as cold.

Darkness was dropping like a blanket about her and she looked longingly towards the cleft in the rock wall that divided this cove from the public one beyond. The man was some distance away now lighting another cigarette, and he probably thought she would need time to dry herself before dressing.

Christina hesitated only a moment before picking up her sandals and sprinting towards the rocks. Her feet made no sound on the soft sand, and the muted roar of the waves disguised her heavy breathing. But in spite of that, every minute she expected him to appear behind her, reaching for her like some avenging god.

She reached the rocks and slid into the crevice, emerging on to the beach beyond. She could see the lights of the harbour now, and she ran towards the jetty swiftly, not stopping to put on her sandals until she had scrambled on to the rough concrete of the harbour wall.

CHAPTER TWO

By the time she reached the Hotel Inglês, Christina had herself in control again, and the nervous trembling had almost disappeared. It was ridiculous, she told herself, allowing one man to disturb her so, and yet there had been something frighteningly intense about that encounter, and she didn't dare to consider what his reactions to her disappearance might be.

The tables on the forecourt of the hotel had been cleared now, and lights gleamed from all the windows. There was music, too, emanating from the general direction of the bar, and the sound of men's voices. Christina entered the hall gratefully. Even Sheila's maliciousness was preferable to what had happened down there on the beach.

She stood hesitatingly in the hall, wondering where Bruce might be, and even as she moved in the direction of the passage leading to their private rooms Bruce himself appeared from the bar, followed closely by her sister-in-law.

'*Christina!*' he exclaimed, and she saw that there was a look of strain about his eyes. 'Where the hell have you been? We've been worried sick!'

Christina made a helpless gesture. 'I'm sorry,' she was beginning, when Sheila burst out:

'You see! I told you she'd be all right. She didn't even consider we'd be at all perturbed at her disappearance! Why is your hair wet, Christina? Surely you haven't been swimming while we've been worrying——'

'That will do, Sheila!' Bruce looked wearily at his sister. 'Well, Christina? Where have you been? Do you realise you've been gone almost two hours?'

Christina ran a hand over her damp hair. 'I am sorry, Bruce, truly, I am. I didn't realise it was so late.'

'But where have you been? You can't have been swimming without a bathing suit. Why is your hair wet? It hasn't been raining.'

Christina sighed. 'It's a long story, Bruce——'

'What she means is, she has been swimming!' Sheila accused, triumphantly. 'I told you, Bruce, she doesn't fit in here. Porto Cedro isn't Faro! We're just beginning to make headway here——'

'Sheila, please!' Bruce hunched his shoulders tiredly. 'Leave this to me. I'm sure Christina must be hungry. She hasn't had a thing since she arrived and knowing her I doubt whether she stopped to eat en route.'

Sheila stared at him. 'You want me to make her something?' she asked resentfully.

'Well, Maria's long gone, hasn't she?' Bruce ran a hand round the back of his neck. 'Sheila, please—do as I ask.'

Sheila shrugged, but with ill grace she went to do as she was bidden and Bruce indicated that Christina should follow him. They went round the reception desk into a small office behind and after the door was closed Bruce looked at her reproachfully.

'Well?' he said. 'I want the truth now. Where have you been all this time?'

Christina thrust her hands awkwardly into her pockets. 'Oh, Bruce!' she said helplessly.

'I want to know, Christina.'

She heaved a sigh. 'Well, all right. I—I—er—went swimming, like Sheila said.'

'My God!' Bruce raised his eyes heavenward. 'Haven't you any more sense than that, Christina?'

Christina coloured defensively. 'I was hot. And I couldn't come back here, could I?'

Bruce shook his head impatiently. 'You could have. You needn't have left at all. Not the hotel, at least. You could have sat outside and waited until I came out to you.'

Christina bent her head. 'I was bored,' she said. 'And the lights attracted me.'

Bruce lit another cigarette. 'You do realise you could have been molested—or arrested!' he observed sombrely.

Christina turned away. Now was the moment to tell her brother what had happened, but she found she couldn't. He seemed to have accepted that she had been swimming from the public beach and she didn't want to disabuse him. To do so would create a whole series of new arguments. So she said nothing and Bruce puffed grimly at his cigarette and then said:

'Well, I suppose I'll have to tell Sheila she was right. But you do realise this will only make matters worse so far as she's concerned?'

'Yes, I realise that.' Christina sighed again. 'Look, Bruce, I meant what I said before. I'll go back to England. I can easily get a job——'

'No, you won't.' Bruce ground his cigarette out in an ashtray. 'I sometimes wonder how you manage to get by without running yourself into serious trouble. You're so—so——'

'Irresponsible!' inserted Christina dryly. 'Yes, I know. But honestly, Bruce, I don't mean to be, I saw no harm——'

'No harm!' Bruce cut her off sharply. 'If I let you go back to England now I'll spend the rest of the summer vacation wondering where you are and who you're with.'

Christina flushed. 'You make me sound like a liability.'

Bruce half smiled. 'Perhaps you are, at that.'

Christina looked at him appealingly. 'Why didn't you tell me Sheila didn't know anything about your invitation?'

Bruce looked discomfited now. 'Oh, Sheila's all right. I've just got to present her with the *fait accompli*, that's all, or she makes so many complaints that I eventually end up by changing my mind. Besides, I had thought you could be of some assistance here.'

'But I can!' Christina's features brightened considerably. 'I told Sheila when I arrived. I'd do anything— wash dishes, make beds, anything! I don't mind working. I shall enjoy it.' Then she frowned. 'But not if Sheila's going to make—make—well, things difficult for you.'

Bruce shrugged. 'I can take it, I guess. In any case, that's what's going to be, so she'll have to accept it.' Then he hesitated. 'But maybe some of what she says is good sense. Tonight, for instance. You could have offended the local population if anyone had seen you, and you do tend to act first and think later. Portugal is still a rather masculine-dominated society, and women are expected to behave with decorum. The way you dress, too. It's not very feminine, is it? Don't you have any skirts—or dresses?'

Christina looked down at her worn jeans. 'Yes, I have dresses. I make my own, mostly. But quite honestly, Bruce, I'm more at home in trousers. I never wear anything else back—back——'

She had been about to say back home, when it suddenly occurred to her with rather shattering poignancy that there was no back home any more. There was back in England, or back at the university, but that was all.

Bruce seemed to sense her sudden remorse, for he moved towards the door, swinging it open and saying: 'Come on! Sheila should have that supper made by now. I'll show you round the hotel tomorrow. I guess tonight all you need is something to eat and then bed!'

Christina's room overlooked the sub-tropical brilliance of the walled garden at the back of the hotel. It was not a large room, but it was attractively furnished with light walnut and apricot coverings and curtains. Obviously all the rooms at the front of the hotel overlooking the sweep of beach and ocean were reserved for paying guests, but Christina didn't mind. The scents from the garden floated in through her open windows and she could hear the sea even if she couldn't see it.

The morning after her arrival, she awoke with a feeling of something ominous hanging over her head, but the feeling dispersed as she washed and dressed and did her hair. It was early in the morning, only a little after six-thirty, but the air was warm and the entrancingly blue sky was an open invitation to be outdoors which Christina could not resist.

Heeding Bruce's kindly remonstrances, she dressed in a plain shift of periwinkle poplin and she secured the long weight of her hair with an elastic band. As she seldom wore make-up her skin was smooth and she knew that in a few days the sun would begin to tan her a golden brown. She had not the usual fair skin that went with her hair, and in consequence the sun did not burn her. The skirt of her dress was absurdly short, but that was something she could not help, and she only hoped Sheila would appreciate the change of attire too much to notice details.

Downstairs she found a young man sweeping in the dining room, and he looked up with interest at her appearance. '*Bom dia, menina!*' he said cheerfully.

Christina smiled. He was a very handsome young man, and it was a relief to meet someone who did not immediately disapprove of her. *'Bom dia,'* she answered his greeting. 'You—you must be Julio.'

'Esta bem, menina.' The young man nodded. 'And you are Senhor Ashley's sister, *sim?'*

'Yes.' Christina was relieved that he spoke English even if his accent was rather pronounced. 'It's a lovely morning, isn't it?'

'A lovely morning,' he repeated slowly. *'Sim, menina, muito formoso!'* A smile spread over his face. 'You are here to stay long?'

Christina shrugged. 'Maybe.' She glanced round. 'You start work very early.'

Julio leant lazily on his brush. *'Sim,* I start early. But then I am free later in the morning.'

'Ah!' Christina nodded understandingly. 'And then what do you do?'

Julio narrowed his eyes. 'Many things, *menina.* Sometimes I swim—sometimes I go out in the boat. Senhor Ashley—your brother—and I sometimes go—how do you say it—skin-diving, *sim?'*

'Do you? How super!' Christina was enthusiastic. 'Does Bruce have a boat?'

Julio nodded. 'A small one, *menina.* Do you skin-dive, also?'

Christina shook her head laughingly. 'Not yet. But I'd like to learn.'

'Perhaps you would permit me to teach you?' Julio's eyes were eloquent with meaning, and Christina felt excitement bubbling up inside her. She could not remain subdued for long, and already the morning which had seemed so foreboding when she awoke had brightened considerably.

Last night when she had gone to bed she had found herself wishing she had never agreed to come here in the first place. Sheila's antagonism had been like a tangible wall of opposition, and she had felt certain that nothing could alter the situation.

29

But now, this morning, with the sun spreading its warmth over the magnificent sweep of sea and shore-line visible through the open door of the hotel, and Julio's undeniable attraction, Christina began to feel entirely different.

'Perhaps you could,' she responded now, in answer to Julio's question, and they shared a mutual smile of anticipation.

'I suggest you get on with your work, Julio!' snapped a brittle voice behind them, and Christina swung round to face her sister-in-law.

'Oh—good morning, Sheila,' she murmured uncomfortably. 'Isn't it a marvellous morning?'

Sheila raised her eyebrows indifferently. 'I haven't had time to notice,' she commented brusquely. 'Now—if you'll come with me, Christina, I'll find you something to do, and introduce you to Maria, our cook.'

Christina cast one lingering glance at the vista outside before shrugging her shoulders resignedly. Julio, turning back to his own chores, closed one eye deliberately, and a smile tugged at the corners of her mouth before she followed Sheila down the hall to a door at the far end.

They entered an enormous kitchen. It was partially tiled and spotlessly clean, with many modern amenities. A rotund Portuguese woman of indeterminate age was in the process of taking a tray of newly baked rolls out of the oven as they entered, and she beamed cheerfully as she placed the tray on the scrubbed wooden table in the centre of the room. The rolls smelt delicious, and Christina's mouth watered in anticipation.

'*Bom dia*, Maria!' said Sheila coolly. 'This is Senhor Ashley's sister. She's come to help us for a while.'

Maria nodded smilingly, but Christina didn't altogether care for Sheila's method of introduction. It seemed obvious that so far as her sister-in-law was concerned, she was to be treated in exactly the same way as the other employees.

Now Sheila looked round, seemed satisfied with what she could see, and went on: 'I'll leave Menina Christina with you, Maria. After she's had something to eat, perhaps you could give her something to do. Preparing breakfast trays—something like that?'

'*Sim, senhora.*' Maria was polite.

'Good.' Sheila nodded and walked to the door. 'I expect I'll see you later, Christina.'

Christina didn't bother to make any comment. Sheila expected none, and besides, what could she say that had not already been said? So she merely nodded, and after Sheila had gone she looked expectantly at the cook.

'You are hungry, *menina*?' Maria's face was never long without a smile. It was evident from the upward tilt of her wide mouth and the laughter lines beside her eyes.

Now Christina nodded eagerly. 'Starving,' she agreed, smiling in return. 'Do you think I could have some coffee and rolls?'

'Why not?' Maria moved to the dresser which stood against one wall and came back with a dish of yellow butter and some plates. 'There you are, *menina*.' She moved back to the stove. 'I will make the coffee.'

The meal that followed was one of the most delicious Christina had ever had. Maria's rolls were light and crisp, oozing with butter, while the coffee was strong and creamy. Maria sat with her while she ate, having coffee, and watching her with obvious satisfaction.

'You *English*!' She shook her head. 'You are so thin! You do not eat the good food there, I think.'

Christina wiped her mouth. 'In England it's considered a crime for a woman to be fat.'

'So?' Maria shook her head impatiently. 'Me—I am always like this. Since I am a young girl, I have always

31

these—these—*dimensaos*!'

'Proportions,' put in Christina smilingly. 'Yes, but then it suits you. It would not suit me to be like you.'

'There is no fear of that, *menina*. While you are here I think I do my best to put a little flesh on those bones, *sim*?'

Christina laughed. 'I'm sure I shall if I have many breakfasts like this,' she said. 'Oh, could I have just one more cup of coffee? That was marvellous!'

After breakfast, Christina helped Maria lay the trays ready to be taken into the dining room to serve the breakfast. Maria told her there were twelve guests in the hotel which meant it was filled to capacity. There were no young children, she said, but there were two boys with their parents as well as several couples. The hotel only catered for bed and breakfast and consequently the guests were out for most of the day, coming back in the evenings sometimes to drink at the bar.

Christina wondered whether she would be expected to serve in the dining room, but she was disabused of this assumption when Sheila returned and summoned her upstairs to help her change the beds of two couples who were leaving that morning.

Unlike while she had been helping Maria, Sheila worked in silence, but whether this was a sullen rejection of Christina's presence or merely her normal way of going about things, Christina could not be sure.

Downstairs again, Bruce was sitting at the reception desk and Christina greeted him warmly.

'Where have you been?' he asked, glancing at his watch. 'It's barely nine.'

Christina chuckled. 'You may not believe this, but I've been up since before seven. I've had breakfast with Maria, helped to lay the breakfast trays, and changed the beds with Sheila.'

'Good God!' Bruce shook his head impatiently.

'Sheila certainly doesn't believe in wasting time. Tell me, how do you feel this morning? Happier about everything? I know last night must have been pretty much of an anti-climax for you.'

Christina touched his hand gently. 'I'm fine, Bruce, really, I am. And I don't mind helping. I shall enjoy it.'

Bruce rose to his feet. 'I'm glad. But if you've been up and about since early this morning I should take it easy now. You don't want to overdo it and the heat can be quite enervating. The main rush of the day is over. Why don't you go out and take a look round the village?'

Christina's eyes twinkled. 'Is that permitted?'

Bruce grinned. 'I don't see why not. You're suitably attired. But if I can get these accounts finished, I'll come with you, if you like.'

'Could you?' Christina nodded eagerly, and Bruce bent his head, studying the register.

Julio appeared from the bar just then. 'I have finished, *senhor!*' he said, his eyes flickering over Christina with interest.

Bruce looked up. 'Fine, Julio. By the way, did that crate of special lager arrive?'

'This morning, *senhor*. With the other delivery.'

'Good.' Bruce nodded. Have you been introduced to my sister?'

Julio smiled. 'We met earlier, *senhor.*'

'Did you?' Bruce considered them both for a few seconds, and then he shrugged. 'Okay, Julio, you can go. Be back around twelve.'

'*Obrigado, senhor.*' Julio inclined his head politely, and walked towards the door with lithe easy strides.

Christina watched him go half-regretfully. She would have liked to have suggested that Julio might show her around, but perhaps he had other commitments.

Bruce watched her expression frowningly. 'I shan't be long,' he said, drawing her attention back to himself, and Christina sighed and nodded, before walking slowly outside.

The sun hit her like a tangible force, the heat burning through the thin poplin of her dress. She longed to be able to go indoors again and collect her swimsuit and spend the morning on the beach. But somehow she sensed that this was not what Bruce had in mind. Was that what Julio intended to do?

She walked out of the forecourt of the hotel and across to the cliff edge, looking down on the harbour below. Away to the right the rocky promontory which guarded the private beach beyond from the public sector looked grim and forbidding. From here it was impossible to discern any breach in its defences, and she sighed again.

Last night, exhaustion had played its part and she had slept dreamlessly, but this morning she was wide awake and everything that had happened down there came back to her with piercing clarity. She could not help but wonder who the man was who lived beyond the headland, who owned that wild and beautiful stretch of shoreline, who had been so badly disfigured by that jagged scar. And yet she did not dare to ask, for to do so would arouse the kind of speculation she did not want to arouse. No one was aware that she knew of that private beach, let alone its owner.

She frowned. The whole interlude had a dreamlike quality somehow. Maybe it had all been a figment of her imagination.

But she knew it had not, and a disturbing finger of apprehension ran down her spine when she considered that she might well meet the man again.

Bruce came out to her just then looking slightly harassed. 'Two of the guests who are leaving this morning want me to drive them to Lagos,' he said. 'I'm sorry, but we'll have to leave our tour of the village until later.'

Christina looked disappointed. 'Couldn't I come to Lagos with you?' she asked.

Bruce shook his head. 'Sheila wants to come to collect some groceries, and the Land-Rover only takes four. Oh, I guess you could sit in the back with the luggage, but——'

'It's all right, Bruce, I understand,' Christina smiled. 'I'll stay here and look after the hotel.'

'That's not necessary, Chris! Maria's quite capable of dealing with anything that comes up. Look, why don't you walk down to the harbour? We should be back in an hour or so.'

Christina frowned. 'All right.'

'You're sure you don't mind?' Bruce looked anxious.

Christina shook her head. 'Of course not. Drive carefully!'

She sat at a table on the hotel forecourt as Bruce got out the Land-Rover from the garage at the back of the building. The guests came out, suitcases, water-skiing equipment, bags and guide books stowed into the vehicle. They smiled at Christina. They were a young married couple, and Christina wondered what the other guests were like. Until now she had felt no desire to find out.

Sheila emerged, sleek and attractive, in a white pleated skirt and a silk overblouse. She glanced casually in Christina's direction and Christina smiled, determined not to show malice. Sheila's eyes flickered, but that was all. And then they were gone, Bruce calling goodbye, and the Land-Rover kicking up a cloud of dust until they turned the corner and disappeared from view.

Christina wrinkled her nose and looked down at her fingernails. Obviously there was nothing Sheila wanted her to do or she would have said so. But now that she was at liberty to do what she liked, to go indoors and get her swimsuit and spend the morning on the beach, the inclination had left her.

She sighed, wishing there was someone she could talk to. Then she thought of Maria. Maria would talk to her. And maybe from her she would be able to glean a little knowledge about the other inhabitants of Porto Cedro.

But when she opened the kitchen door, Maria was not alone. Julio was there, perched on the edge of the table, in the process of eating a newly peeled peach. He slid off the table at her entrance and Christina stood there, rather disconcerted by the admiring look in his eyes.

'I'm sorry, Maria,' she said. 'I thought you might be alone.'

Maria waved her hands. 'Do not mind Julio, *menina*,' she exclaimed cheerfully. 'He is on his way, are you not, Julio?'

'If you say so, *mae minha*!' remarked Julio good-naturedly.

Christina frowned. 'Julio is your son, Maria?'

'*Sim, menina*. Did not the *senhora* tell you so?'

'No, she didn't.' Christina shook her head. 'Where are you going, Julio?' There was a wistful note in her voice now.

Julio threw the peach stone away and wiped his hands on a cloth at the sink. 'I am going down to the harbour. My uncle has a boat. I am going to help him paint it.'

Maria frowned at him. 'You are not polite, *menino*!' she said sharply, speaking in English for Christina's benefit. 'The *menina* has a name!'

'Oh, please!' Christina was embarrassed. 'I—I'd like you both to call me Christina, that's all. I—well, I'm not used to being called miss, or anything like that. Christina is fine, really!'

Maria heaved a sigh. 'And the *senhora*? Your sister-in-law? She would approve of this, *menina*?'

Christina looked mutinous. 'Does it matter?'

Maria spread her hands. 'I should say so, *sim*.'

Christina lifted her shoulders and then let them fall dejectedly. 'What does it matter? A name is just a name. If you ask me, things are far too formal here!'

Julio laughed, ignoring his mother's scandalised face. 'I agree—Christina. And I will use your name. At least, when we are alone.'

'*Julio!*' His mother's voice was a warning.

Julio raised his dark eyebrows, his eyes glinting with mockery. 'Perhaps—Christina—would like to come down to paint Tio Ramon's boat with me.'

Christina's eyes danced. 'Could I?'

Maria's lips were pursed. 'Julio, she cannot, and you know it.'

'Why not? Why can't I?' Christina stared at the cook appealingly.

'Your brother—and the *senhora*—they would not approve.'

'But they're not here!'

'They will not be long.' Maria was adamant.

Julio shrugged regretfully. 'You see,' he said. 'It is the way.'

'Well, it's not my way,' exclaimed Christina impatiently. 'Good heavens, I'm English! Not Portuguese!'

Maria shrugged her ample shoulders. 'These are not my rules, *menina*,' she said.

Julio hesitated by the door. 'I will see you later in the day, Christina.'

Christina hunched her shoulders. 'Oh, I suppose so.'

He went out, and after he had gone, Christina moved about restlessly, fingering a plate here, a saucepan there, impatient and defiant, and yet unable to take the step that would put her yet again in Sheila's disfavour, and cause more trouble for Bruce.

Maria put some dirty dishes into the sink and began to run hot water upon them. She glanced round at Christina sympathetically. 'Why don't you go for a walk, *menina*? The village is small. You won't get lost.'

Christina sighed. 'I suppose I could.'

'Of course. And soon your brother will be back from Lagos.'

Christina nodded, and with a smile of resignation she left the kitchen, walking along the hall to the front door. Two men were sitting outside at one of the tables, looking at some maps. They looked up as she passed them, saying something in their own language which she thought was German. But they were older men, well into their forties, and they held no interest for her.

She looked down the road to the harbour. Julio had gone and she presumed he was already down there, and she envied him. On impulse, she walked down the steep road to the harbour and crossing to the wall she looked down on the shingle that edged the jetty now that the tide was out.

She saw Julio and his uncle at once. They were sitting on an upturned boat, having a cigarette before starting work, and Julio, looking up, saw her immediately. He said something to his uncle, who nodded, and then he bounded across the sand to her side. In denim jeans and an openwork sweater of a faded shade of blue, he was very attractive, and she could not help smiling at him.

He looked up at her, leaning on the wall above him and said: 'What are you doing? Playing truant?'

Christina's lips parted. 'I'm tempted. Is that your uncle?'

'Yes. Come and meet him?'

'Should I?'

'Why not?' Julio's dark eyes were amused.

'All right.' Christina swung her legs over the wall, and Julio lifted her down on to the sand, his fingers lingering a moment longer than was necessary at her waist. She was very conscious of him, too. It was the normal healthy consciousness of any young woman for any young man and she felt no sense of embarrassment now at the warmth in his eyes.

Julio's uncle was a garrulous old man, but as he spoke mostly in his own language Christina could understand very little. The job of painting his boat seemed of little importance compared with the chance to gossip and time passed swiftly as other fishermen came to be introduced and smiled appreciatively at the attractive young English girl with her mane of corn-gold hair, and long slender legs.

At last Christina was forced to look at her watch and she saw it was already after eleven. 'I must go,' she said to Julio quickly, and he nodded.

'I'll walk back with you,' he said. 'Surely my mother will see no harm in that.'

As the road flattened out at the head of the slope from the harbour, Christina saw a huge car outside her brother's hotel, and parked a little ahead of it, the Land-Rover.

'Your brother has visitors,' remarked Julio dryly, and Christina felt her nerves stretch a little. The black limousine was familiar. It was the car which had passed her the day before on the road from Lagos. The car with the insignia on the side; the car which belonged to ... She swallowed hard. He had not actually said it was his car, but ...

Julio noticed her anxious expression, and smiled. 'Do not look so anxious, Christina. It is merely the car of your brother's—how do you say it—*dono, senhorio*?'

Christina frowned. 'You mean—Bruce's landlord?'

'Ah, *sim*, that is the word I have heard Senhor Ashley use. Landlord!'

39

Christina's nerves tightened. 'But what is he doing here?'

Julio shrugged. 'Who knows? Is it *importante*?'

'I suppose not.' Christina stiffened her shoulders and bidding Julio goodbye she crossed the road and walked past the magnificent Mercedes with its insignia and crest, the words of which she could read now: *Fiel ate Morte*—Faithful until Death.

The hall of the hotel was shadowy after the brilliance of the sunlight outside, but she could hear voices in the lounge. She would have liked to have walked straight past, but Bruce had seen her shadow and he came to the door of the lounge and said: 'Come in, Christina. We were beginning to think you'd disappeared again.'

Christina hesitated in the doorway of the lounge, but the man who was standing in the middle of the floor talking to Sheila was not the scarred man she had met on the beach the night before. He was an older man, fifty at least, with greying dark hair, and rather nice brown eyes. He wore a dark uniform however, and carried a flat hat, and Christina realised that he was the chauffeur. Would he recognise her?

Bruce smiled at his sister now, and said: 'This is Alfredo Seguin, Christina. Alfredo, I'd like to introduce you to my sister. She's come to stay with us for a while.'

Alfredo Seguin looked at Christina and for a moment something flickered in the depths of his eyes, and then he smiled and said: 'I am delighted to make your acquaintance, Miss Ashley. I hope you will enjoy your stay in the Algarve.'

'Thank you.' Christina's reply was stilted.

'And now I must be going.' Alfredo was reluctant. 'Thank you for that most excellent coffee, Mrs. Ashley. *Ate logo*, Miss Ashley—*senhor!*'

Bruce escorted the man to the door and Christina

stood for a moment looking after them, biting her lips. Sheila, unaware of her sister-in-law's discomposure, said: 'Where have you been this morning?'

Christina gathered her scattered thoughts. 'Oh—er—just down to the harbour,' she replied honestly. 'Who—who was that man?'

'Alfredo Seguin? He's chauffeur to Dom Carlos.'

'Dom Carlos?' Christina repeated the words slowly.

'Dom Carlos Martinho Duarte de Ramirez, to be exact,' said Bruce ceremoniously, from behind them. 'Lord of all he surveys, and that includes the Hotel Inglês!'

Christina managed a smile. 'I see.'

'Not that you're likely to meet Dom Carlos,' remarked Sheila carelessly. 'Alfredo, and another man—his estate manager, Jorge Vicente—they usually attend to his business affairs.'

Bruce glanced at his watch. 'Time for coffee?' he suggested.

'You've just had coffee!' stated Sheila coolly.

'But Christina hasn't. And I could surely drink some more of that most excellent beverage,' her husband mocked her gently, using Alfredo's words.

Sheila smiled faintly. It was the nearest she had come to good humour in Christina's presence, and Christina felt an overwhelming sense of relief that some things at least were improving. After Sheila had left them, Bruce said: 'Where did you go this morning, Christina?'

'I walked down to the harbour. Tell me something, Bruce, this man—this Dom Carlos—where does he live?'

Bruce frowned. 'Why?'

Christina shrugged lightly. 'I'm interested, that's all. It's not every day one hears of such a person.'

Bruce seemed satisfied with her explanation, for he said: 'He lives at the Quinta Ramirez. His estate.'

41

Christina ran her finger over the surface of the table. 'I suppose that's some distance away,' she ventured probingly.

'Not far. The estate begins just beyond the village. He owns most of the land hereabouts. The Quinta itself is quite a showplace, I'm told. Naturally I've never been there.'

'Why naturally?'

Bruce smiled. 'Men like Ramirez don't mix with people like us. Besides, I believe he doesn't encourage social callers.'

'But you have met him?'

'Oh, yes. At the time I leased the hotel, I met him at his office in Faro, and since I've seen him a couple of times. Why? Why this curiosity about a man you're never likely to meet?'

Christina coloured. 'Just feminine inquisitiveness, I suppose,' she replied, realising she could not go on asking questions. But Bruce had not said the one thing which would have identified Dom Carlos once and for all as the man she had encountered on the beach.

Sheila returned with the tray of coffee and placed it on the low table and Christina suppressed all thoughts of the man. Besides, what did it matter? No doubt Dom Carlos, if that indeed was his name, had forgotten all about her by now.

During the afternoon, Bruce took Christina on her promised tour of the village, finishing at the harbour where Bruce's boat, *Fantasma*, was moored. There were several tourists down at the harbour looking at the boats, but although this was the height of the season there was none of the commercialisation in Porto Cedro that could be found further along the coast. Christina wondered how long it would remain unspoilt, but when she mentioned her doubts to Bruce, he replied:

'So long as Dom Carlos wants it this way, it will stay

as it is. He owns the land. If he doesn't sell, the developers can't build their ghastly concrete monstrosities that they call hotels in Porto Cedro.'

Christina was tempted to use the opening to ask more questions, but something distracted her attention and the moment passed.

After the evening meal, she was glad to sit in the lounge of the hotel until bedtime. It had been an extraordinarily exhausting day and she decided to go to bed soon after nine o'clock. But although she was tired she could not sleep. Thoughts of the man from the beach haunted her. How did he come to be scarred so dreadfully? What kind of experience had been responsible for that disfiguration that was at once ugly and attractive? What kind of effect had it had on his life? His family? Was he married? Did he have any children of his own? He could have, quite easily. She judged his age to be somewhere between thirty-five and forty-five, but it was difficult to be certain.

She sighed. It was crazy lying here pondering over a man who had treated her with nothing but arrogance and contempt, and yet her naturally responsive nature would not allow her to bear malice for long and she was passionately curious to learn more about him.

The next morning, she bathed before seven, returning to the hotel before Sheila had chance to comment on her non-appearance. Julio looked at her wet hair reproachfully as she came in.

'You did not tell me,' he said, indicating the swimsuit dangling wetly from her fingers. 'I would have come with you.'

Christina smiled. 'I didn't think your mother would approve!' she taunted him.

'I approve—and that is what counts,' he murmured insistently, and she laughed and went up to her room.

Later in the morning, Sheila sent her to the market to buy some fresh fruit. Clad in her poplin dress, her

43

still damp hair secured with an elastic band, a basket on her arm, she felt she mingled well with the other Portuguese women there, but she was unaware that her golden colouring could not help but distinguish her from the crowd.

She was considering the price of melons when there was a murmur about her, and she looked round in surprise, wondering what had disturbed everyone. A tall man was making his way between the stalls coming in her direction, nodding and giving an occasional smile to the people he passed. The women in the crowd drew back respectfully, pulling their children out of his path so that Christina was reminded of peasants in the presence of royalty. But it was the man himself who imprisoned her attention, a lean, dark man, dressed immaculately in a navy silk suit with a matching navy shirt and tie. And as he neared Christina her stomach muscles tightened as she saw again the livid scar on his tanned cheek.

She lifted her startled eyes and met his curiously light ones, and as her nerves tingled she noticed the length and thickness of his lashes. He had recognised her, she knew, and she turned to the stallholder with almost desperate urgency, asking the price of the melons.

'*Momento, menina,*' he exclaimed, almost scandalised that she should expect him to serve her when obviously someone of importance was approaching.

Christina turned away, pushing through the throng carelessly, only wanting to avoid a further encounter. But her pursuer had the advantage, she soon found, for his way was made clear for him while she had to force a pathway.

'*Menina!*' The curt tone of his voice halted her, and she was intensely conscious of the curious speculation around her.

Sighing, she turned slowly to face him, and he inclined his head in satisfaction. But he said nothing, merely passed her and indicated that she should follow him.

Unwillingly Christina complied, for she had the distinct feeling that had she attempted to disobey him these people would have forcibly made her do exactly as he had indicated.

Outside the throng of humanity, he halted and now she could see the black limousine parked in the square, Alfredo Seguin at the wheel. He must have noticed her eyes move past him to the automobile, for a cynical expression invaded his eyes. She could see his eyes clearly now, and they were a most peculiar tawny colour, sometimes palest amber, sometimes almost yellow around the irises.

'So we meet again, *menina*,' he observed, his accent more pronounced than she remembered.

CHAPTER THREE

CHRISTINA held the basket almost defensively in front of her, both hands gripping the handle tightly. 'Yes, *senhor*!' she responded automatically, more calmly than she felt. All of a sudden she could feel the panic which had assailed her the other evening on the beach when confronted by his almost sinister attraction, and she wondered what it was about him that disturbed her so. His dark clothes fitted him so well, while she was intensely conscious of the faded cotton of her dress and the shortness of its skirt.

'And now you know who I am, do you not?' he continued, glancing round meaningfully towards his sleek limousine.

Christina made an indifferent gesture. 'I suppose you must be Dom Carlos Ramirez,' she conceded reluctantly.

He bowed his head in a faintly continental manner. 'That is correct, *menina*. Or perhaps I should say— Miss Ashley? That is your name, is it not? And you are the sister of Senhor Bruce Ashley who runs the Hotel Inglês!'

Christina realised their stilted interchange was being observed by at least twenty pairs of eyes. 'You're very well informed, *senhor*,' she said uncomfortably.

Dom Carlos Ramirez extracted a case of cheroots from his pocket and placed one between his teeth, supremely indifferent to their audience. 'You will find, *menina*, that I am well informed about most things,' he said, lighting the cheroot with a slim gold lighter.

Christina moved restlessly, remembering that she had not yet got the melons for Sheila. 'If you'll excuse me, *senhor*, I must go. My sister-in-law is expecting me back.'

Dom Carlos regarded her intently, exhaling aromatic smoke into the air above her head. 'Why did you run away from me?' he demanded quietly, ignoring her protest with cool dismissal.

Christina lifted her slim shoulders helplessly. 'I was —trespassing——'

'So? Were you perhaps afraid I might call the *policia*?'

'Of course not.' Christina resented his assumption that she must have been afraid.

'Then was it this that repulsed you so?' He flicked a careless hand at his cheek, and Christina felt a wave of hot colour sweeping up her throat.

'No, I——' she began awkwardly, when he held up a silencing hand.

'Do not be afraid to admit it. I realise my appearance must present an alarming spectacle to anyone unused to it. These people here——' He glanced round carelessly. 'They are used to me—to my, shall we say, unsightliness—and I forget that others are not prepared——'

'That's not true!' Christina stared at him hotly.

Dom Carlos again ignored her outburst. 'But I also regret what happened. I mistook you for one of these indolent young people who have time only to waste— to do little but make nuisances of themselves. What is it you English call them? Beatniks? *Hippies?*' He shook his head. 'It is of no account. I am told you are merely on holiday here, and your actions the other evening were no doubt the result of overcharged exuberance.'

Christina felt a rising sense of frustration. He was so cool, so detached, so much the master of the situation.

He was treating her in much the same way as he would treat any irresponsible infant, and it was infuriating. Did he think she was a child just out of the schoolroom?

She looked up at him impatiently. She was a tall girl and normally she was on eye level terms with the boys of her acquaintance, but Dom Carlos's height and presence immediately put her at a disadvantage.

'Whether I'm on holiday or not is immaterial, *senhor*,' she said shortly. 'Your attitudes towards young people are still dated. And contrary to your suppositions, hippies are not all immoral layabouts, and I admire them for choosing a different way of life——'

Dom Carlos smiled, but it did not quite reach those strange cat's eyes. 'Come,' he said. 'I will escort you back to the hotel.'

Christina mentally shook him away. 'I'm perfectly capable of seeing myself back to the hotel,' she said. 'Besides, I promised to get some melons for Sheila.'

Dom Carlos raised his dark eyebrows sardonically. 'Maybe you could purchase these melons at some other time,' he suggested suavely.

Christina looped the basket over her arm. 'Why not now?'

Dom Carlos ground the butt of his cheroot beneath an elegantly shod heel. 'Because I wish to speak with your brother, and now is as good a time as any, *menina*.'

Christina stiffened. 'Do you intend to tell him about —about—the other evening?'

Dom Carlos cupped the smooth skin of her elbow with one hard brown hand, and she quivered at the disturbing pressure of his skin against hers. But he seemed not to notice, for he propelled her forward deliberately, saying: 'You have not told him yourself, I perceive.'

Christina was forced to move with him and she

heard the engine of the limousine fire, and presently the drone of its motor as it cruised a few yards behind them.

'I—I didn't think it was important,' she retorted heatedly.

Dom Carlos inclined his head towards her, and they turned out of the square into the narrow footway that led through to the seafront. Christina was glad to be out of sight of so many curious eyes, and she was amazed that he should have chosen to speak to her in front of his people.

The limousine cruised past the end of the footway to take the wider road, and for several moments they were completely alone. But although Christina felt a choking sensation in her throat, Dom Carlos was completely composed and when they emerged into the sunlight he said: 'Do not be alarmed, *menina*. I do not carry tales.'

Christina pulled away from him. It was galling to know that he was able to arouse a disturbing sense of awareness inside her when he so obviously remained completely unmoved. But then he regarded her merely as an annoying child, that was all.

The limousine was parked outside the hotel as they approached and Dom Carlos bent to its window and said something to Alfredo, who nodded and touched his cap politely. Then he was following Christina indoors, and she felt an ominous feeling of foreboding.

Bruce was at the reception desk as they entered and he rose to his feet in surprise when he recognised his illustrious guest.

'Why—Dom Carlos!' he exclaimed. 'Is something wrong?' His gaze flickered anxiously to Christina, and she made an impatient grimace of dismissal.

Dom Carlos unbuttoned the jacket of his lounge suit and after shaking hands with Bruce slid his hands into his trousers pockets. 'Nothing is wrong, *meu amigo*! I encountered your young sister in the market place and as I wished to speak with you I escorted her home.'

Christina made as though to leave them, when the Dom's voice halted her. 'Perhaps your brother would allow you to drive with me later to the Quinta Ramirez,' he said, taking her breath away by his cool invitation that was so unexpected. 'There you may pick some melons for your sister-in-law, *sim*?'

Christina looked helplessly at Bruce, who gave a little involuntary shake of his head, as though he didn't quite understand any of this. Taking her cue from her brother, Christina said: 'Thank you, *senhor*, but I can go to the market later——'

'But I insist.' Dom Carlos's smile never faltered, but there was an implacability about him which was unmistakable. 'Until later, *menina*!'

Christina managed a slight gesture of assent and then hastened down the hall towards the kitchen. She hadn't the faintest idea why Dom Carlos Ramirez, who had apparently never visited the Hotel Inglês, should have suddenly taken it into his head to visit her brother, and she wondered with a sinking sense of unease what Sheila would make of it all.

But what could she make of it? What could any of them make of it? And certainly there was no getting near Dom Carlos to find out until he was prepared to inform them. As she remembered the conversation she had just had with him resentment flared. He had deliberately ignored everything she had said which did not conform to his beliefs with an aloof indifference that typified the man. It was as though it was impossible to penetrate the façade he presented to the world, and she wondered how anyone could reach the real man behind the mask.

She heard Bruce inviting Dom Carlos into the office and then the door closed behind them and there was silence. With a sigh, she pushed open the kitchen door and entered the warm comfortable atmosphere of Maria's domain.

Sheila was there, drinking coffee, flicking through the pages of a magazine, and she looked up impatiently as Christina entered the room.

'Well?' she said. 'Did you get them?'

Christina stood down her basket on the table. 'No,' she replied reluctantly.

'No?' Sheila shut the magazine. 'Why?'

Christina sighed. 'I met Dom Carlos Ramirez in the market square. He—he escorted me home.'

Sheila could not have looked more incredulous and had it not all been so serious Christina could have laughed at her expression. 'You did what?' she whispered faintly.

Christina shrugged. 'I've told you. I met Dom Carlos Ramirez——'

'Yes—yes! But how? How did he know who you were?'

Christina tried to control her colour. 'I don't know,' she said moodily. 'I—I suppose—Alfredo—recognised me!' She heaved a sigh. Alfredo had just that instant come to her mind!

'I see.' Sheila frowned. 'Even so, why should Dom Carlos speak to you?'

'I don't know.' Christina compressed her lips. 'Anyway, he's here now. Talking with Bruce.'

Sheila was scandalised. 'In the hotel?'

'Yes, of course.' Christina was growing impatient with the whole affair. It was bad enough surviving the encounter with Ramirez without having to suffer Sheila's astonished protests.

Sheila looked at Maria who had listened to this interchange in silence. 'What ought I to do, Maria?' she asked urgently. 'Should I take a tray of coffee in to them? Or should I ask first?'

Maria shrugged her ample shoulders. 'Perhaps as it

is almost lunchtime, Dom Carlos would like some wine,' she suggested.

'Wine? Oh, yes, wine!' Sheila spread her hands doubtfully. 'But should I ask first?'

Christina wrinkled her nose. 'Why bother with anything? I'm quite sure Ramirez would look down his aristocratic nose at anything we provided!'

Maria looked shocked now. 'Ah, no, *menina*, that is not so. Dom Carlos is a good man—a kind man—a man much beloved of his people.'

Christina looked sceptical. 'Oh yes? So they live in cottages while good kind Dom Carlos lives in a magnificent house on his estates. Bruce told me. It's quite a showpiece.'

Maria wrung her hands impatiently. 'It is only right that Dom Carlos should live in the house of his ancestors, *menina*. No one would have it otherwise. But he is not like them. He cares for his people. He works unceasingly providing money for schools—hospitals—better working conditions——'

Christina perched on the edge of the table swinging one bare leg. 'Are you his advocate, Maria?' she asked mockingly.

Sheila was ignoring their argument, setting a tray with a fine linen cloth, putting out exquisitely cut glasses.

'Advocate? Advocate? What is this?' Maria said now, confused.

'For goodness' sake, what does it matter?' Sheila looked angrily at Christina. 'Get down off that table, Christina, and start preparing some vegetables. For all we know, Bruce may invite Dom Carlos to stay for lunch.'

Christina slid off her perch and looked at Maria who was muttering bitterly to herself. She touched the older woman's arm gently. She had not realised Maria was taking it so seriously.

'I'm sorry,' she said, while Sheila seethed with impatience.

'Who is going to take the tray through?' she demanded shortly.

'Well, not me,' replied Christina firmly.

Sheila quickly considered her reflection in the mirror by the door. 'Do I look all right, then?'

In a slim-fitting shift of olive green cotton, Sheila looked very attractive and she knew it. But Christina nodded agreeably, and said: 'Of course. You look fine.'

Sheila seemed satisfied, for she patted her hair, lifted the tray and went out. After she had gone Christina gave Maria another appealing smile and then walked over to the stove. The coffee pot was still hot. 'Can I have some?' she asked, looking earnestly at Maria.

Maria hesitated and then she half smiled. '*Sim, sim*, I suppose.' Then she frowned. 'But you do not speak of Dom Carlos in that way again, *menina*. It makes me very angry.'

'All right, I'm sorry.' Christina was placating. 'Hmm, you do make the most delicious coffee, Maria.'

Maria was consoled and they were chatting together amicably a few moments later when Sheila came back, minus the tray. She leaned against the door for a moment after she came in, and stared curiously at Christina, so that Christina herself felt embarrassed by the intensity of that scrutiny.

'Well?' she said awkwardly. 'Was the wine suitable?'

'How do you know Dom Carlos?' snapped Sheila angrily.

Christina stared at her. 'I—I don't know him. I told you—we walked back from the market together this morning——'

Sheila straightened, moving away from the door. 'Then tell me, why are you driving out to the *quinta* with him?'

Christina put down her coffee cup. 'I—I didn't have time to buy the melons, as you know. Dom Carlos suggested I might like to drive back to the *quinta* with him and pick some.' She sighed. 'Well, don't look at me like that. It's the truth. It wasn't my idea.'

Sheila drummed her fingers on the rough table. 'But why? Why couldn't he have allowed you to buy some in the market later? And why is he here? Talking to Bruce?' She pressed her thin lips together. 'I don't understand this at all.'

Christina shook her head, and then glanced musing at Maria. 'Maybe he considers I'm in need of guidance?' she suggested smilingly. 'Maybe I'm to be another of his good works.'

Sheila looked up sharply. 'And why should he think that? What have you done that he should imagine you need guidance?'

Christina coloured now. For a moment she had almost betrayed herself. 'I—I don't know,' she replied awkwardly. 'I—I was joking, that's all.'

Sheila looked at her piercingly, obviously trying to decide for herself whether or not Christina was lying. Then she shrugged and turned away. 'Anyway, if you're going to the *quinta*, I should go and change if I were you. You look an absolute sight in that dress!'

Sheila could not have said anything designed to annoy Christina more. Her patronising tone of voice, coming as it did only minutes after Dom Carlos's condescension, was sufficient to arouse a demon of perversity inside the other girl, and without a word Christina walked out of the kitchen, slamming the door behind her.

In her bedroom, she surveyed her reflection critically in the mirror of her dressing table. It was not true, she told herself indignantly. She did not look a sight. The cotton dress was faded and old, but it was still decent enough to wear. And besides, what did it matter to her what anyone here thought of her? She had never had a lot of money to spend on clothes and her most usual attire was trousers and an anorak. She was completely unaware that Sheila's malice was motivated by jealousy. Admiring her sister-in-law's slim elegance as she did, Christina had never stopped to consider her own attributes. But Sheila was aware of them, and she took every opportunity presented to her to undermine the younger girl's confidence.

Now Christina tore off the offending dress and tugged open the door of her wardrobe. If a dress wasn't suitable, then she would not wear one.

When she came downstairs again she was wearing cream denim trousers and a cream cotton shirt. The masculine attire accentuated the slim curve of her hips while her hair, which she had deliberately left loose, hung straightly about her shoulders. She had been tempted to wear a bandanna, Indian-style, round her forehead, but had finally decided against it even though she knew it suited her.

She hesitated in the hall, unwilling to invade the privacy of her brother's office, but equally unwilling to face Sheila's scandalised objections to her appearance. Julio had heard her footsteps on the stairs and came to lean against the door of the bar, his eyes admiring.

'*Pois bem*,' he murmured consideringly. 'Most attractive. But do you know your brother has an important visitor?'

Christina sighed. 'Ramirez! I know.'

'*Dom* Carlos Ramirez!' remarked Julio dryly. 'Don't forget that.'

Christina made a face at him. 'Why? Is he some kind of god, or something?'

Julio looked mildly taken aback. 'No, but——'

'But nothing! I'm getting a little sick of hearing about him,' retorted Christina heatedly. Then she frowned: 'Tell me something—is he married?'

'Dom Carlos?' Julio shook his head. 'No.'

Christina shrugged. 'I'm surprised. I should have thought all the mamas in the neighbourhood would have practically been camping on his doorstep as he's so eligible!'

Julio smiled. 'Maybe they'd like to. But they'd be wasting their time.'

'Why?' Christina was curious in spite of everything.

Julio spread an eloquent hand. 'Dom Carlos is not interested in women. At least—not now.'

'What do you mean?' Christina stared at him, but at that moment the door to Bruce's office opened and the man they had been discussing emerged, followed closely by Christina's brother.

Christina adopted an indifferent attitude, and Julio disappeared back into the bar, but not before Dom Carlos had observed his presence. Bruce was talking animatedly to their guest, red-faced and obviously still bemused by this visit, but his eyes widened angrily when they encountered Christina's appearance and she realised he would never forgive her for embarrassing him like this.

'Are you ready to leave for the *quinta*, Miss Ashley?' Dom Carlos's dark eyes were assessing her appearance clinically.

Christina nodded. 'If you like,' she agreed, indifferently.

Dom Carlos turned to smile at Bruce. 'Please give my thanks to your wife for the wine,' he said charmingly.

Bruce made a deprecatory gesture. 'It has been an honour, Dom Carlos,' he began awkwardly.

'And you will consider our discussion further?' The Dom regarded him intently. 'You will explain the situation to your wife?'

'Of course, sir,' Bruce nodded vigorously.

'*Esta bem.*' Dom Carlos turned back to Christina.

'Shall we go, *menina*?'

Christina pressed her lips together, looking frustratedly at Bruce. 'All right,' she said in a small voice.

Bruce accompanied them out to the car. Alfredo Seguin emerged hastily to open the door for them, and Dom Carlos indicated that Christina should get in first. She did so with some misgivings and the door was closed securely behind her. Then Dom Carlos walked round to the seat Alfredo had been occupying and took the wheel himself while Alfredo climbed swiftly into the front of the huge car beside him. A hand was raised casually in salute to Bruce, whose face had now assumed a rather anxious expression, and then the car moved smoothly away.

Christina moved restlessly on the massive back seat. She felt ridiculous, sitting there in state, and she wondered whether Dom Carlos had done it deliberately to disconcert her. What was his purpose in bringing her to the *quinta*? What possible interest could he have in whether or not she got melons? It was ludicrous, and quite suddenly she felt an ominous sense of unease. There had to be more to it than she had been told, but what?

The car soon left the environs of the village, following the coast road for a while before turning inland through thickly wooded countryside. They soon reached tall, wrought iron gates that bore the crest of the Ramirez family, and an elderly lodge keeper hurried out to throw the gates wide, saluting the Dom as he did so. They drove through and followed a tree-lined drive, beyond which stretched acres of parkland. In the far distance, orchards of trees could be seen, and as they drove further into the estate Christina saw the sea dropping away to their left.

She had not realised how immense the estate might be, and by the time they reached the *quinta* itself she was positively fascinated. The whole area was a blaze of colour, scarlet hibiscus, pink and white oleanders, banks of poinsettias hedging the road; flowers she had hitherto not seen outside of greenhouses. The air was redolent with their scents and combined with the heat of the day it had a somnolent effect on Christina so that she wished the drive would go on and on . . .

But at last they emerged from a concealing belt of trees and Christina saw the graceful beauty of the Quinta Ramirez ahead of them. The huge car circled a gravelled courtyard containing a stone fountain, which provided the constant cooling sound of running water, and came to rest at the foot of shallow marble steps leading up to a mosaic-tiled terrace.

Christina stared in fascination. She would never have believed that people still inhabited such places. It was so much bigger, so much more imposing than she had ever dreamed that for a moment she was transfixed.

The *quinta* was made of grey stone, mellowed by a thousand seasons, tall Moorish windows shuttered against the glare of the sun. Urns and alabaster jugs spilled semi-tropical shrubs across the terrace, while above the massive front door, the coat of arms of the Ramirez family was carved in stone. Along the terrace itself, exquisite *azulejos* depicted examples of Portugal's turbulent history.

Alfredo came and opened the door and offered his hand to assist her to alight, but Christina climbed out unaided, staring up at the *quinta* for several more minutes before dragging her gaze back to her host.

Dom Carlos had alighted also and was regarding her expression tolerantly. 'You find my home interesting, Miss Ashley?' he queried quietly.

Christina sighed. 'Who wouldn't?' she exclaimed, and then added: 'I mean—of course, Dom Carlos!'

'Good,' he said. 'You will stay to lunch, of course.' He smiled. 'We will be adequately chaperoned by my aunt, Donna Inez, although I suppose the formalities are of little importance to you.'

Christina wanted to protest. Apart from anything else she was not suitably dressed for lunch at the *quinta*, and she was instinctively aware that his remark about a chaperon was a deliberate attempt to appease her desire to be treated as an adult. He did not consider the formalities unimportant, but her behaviour had simply increased his contention that she was hopelessly adolescent.

She looked at him moodily out of the corners of her eyes. Could nothing ever shake that detached and formal façade of his? Was he really as indifferent to life and to people as he appeared?

'I'm not dressed for lunch, *senhor*,' she said now, as they mounted the shallow steps together, hating the feeling of inferiority he created within her.

Dom Carlos seemed amused. 'Oh, I am sure my aunt will not object. And besides, there is someone I want you to meet.'

Christina frowned, and then gasped as they passed through the massive entrance and she found herself in a high-ceilinged hall, the floor of which was tiled in black and white with a magnificent baroque staircase leading up to a grilled gallery. There were flowers everywhere, and the air was heavy with their scent. With difficulty, she dragged her mind back to his words. 'Someone you wish me to meet, *senhor*?' she echoed.

'*Sim, menina.* Come—we will perform the introduction now, before lunch.'

Christina went with him across the tiled hall, through a modern lounge, and out through french doors on to a wide patio at the back of the building. The grey stone walls of the *quinta* provided shade on three sides of the patio, while the centre was taken up by a curving sickle-shaped swimming pool. Its blue

59

depths looked very inviting and Christina looked about her with unconcealed interest. Baskets of flowers were suspended from the gallery of the upper floor which circled this area, and climbing plants wound their sinuous stems about the carved pillars supporting it.

As Christina's step slowed to take in all this beauty, Dom Carlos turned, and said: 'Come, *menina*! Miguel can see us now.'

Christina looked at him frowningly, and then as he turned his head, she looked beyond him to the far side of the patio where, in the shade of the gallery a boy was seated in a wheelchair. Her gaze turned again to her host, but his tawny eyes were suddenly enigmatic and he strode ahead of her round the pool to where the boy was sitting.

As Christina neared them she could hear Dom Carlos speaking to the boy in their own language, and the boy was nodding and looking towards Christina with undisguised curiosity. Christina could see he was thin, painfully so, and his mouth drooped in lines of apathy, his skin sallow beside the darkness of Dom Carlos. And yet, for all that, there was a resemblance. The blue-black hair was the same, and so, too, were the high cheekbones, the finely chiselled lips with the lower lip fuller, almost sensual.

Dom Carlos straightened as she reached them, and he said: 'I'd like you to meet my nephew, *menina*. Miguel, this is Miss Christina Ashley!'

Miguel's thin young face broke into a reluctant smile of welcome. It was as though his innate politeness, the training of years, deemed it necessary for him to show enthusiasm even though he might not feel such enthusiasm. Christina's heart went out to him in that moment.

'Hello, Miguel,' she said, shaking the hand he held out to her.

'*Bom dia, senhorita!*' Miguel was courteous.

Christina judged his age to be perhaps twelve or thirteen, but he had the refinement and composure of a much older boy.

'Miss Ashley is at university in England,' observed his uncle smoothly, disabusing Christina once and for all of her assumption that he thought she was still at school, and she wondered whether he had got his information from Bruce. 'But she is on holiday at the moment, staying with her brother in the village.'

'*Sim*, Tio Carlos!' Miguel nodded. Then he looked at Christina. 'What are you studying, *senhorita*?'

Christina hesitated for a moment, and then she went down on her haunches beside his chair so that she was not continually forcing him to look up at her. 'I'm studying English and history,' she replied, with warmth. 'Do you go to school, Miguel?'

Miguel glanced up at his uncle as though for guidance and then he shook his head. '*Nao, senhorita.* I have a professor who teaches me here, at the *quinta*.'

'I see.' Christina glanced up at Dom Carlos now. 'And do you like learning? What are your favourite subjects?'

Miguel loked interested. 'Oh, yes, *senhorita*, I like to absorb knowledge.' He smiled, more naturally. 'And I enjoy literature most of all. I have read all your most famous writers—Dickens, Henry James, even Shakespeare, although I must confess there are poets I prefer.'

Christina smiled, too. 'I like literature, too,' she said. 'I read an enormous amount, almost anything I can lay my hands on. I have no preferences, so long as the book is well written. I think that is the most important thing—for the writer to be able to get his impressions across to his readers.'

'Oh, yes, I agree,' exclaimed Miguel, with enthusiasm. 'Tell me, *senhorita*, have you read any of our

Portuguese writers?'

Dom Carlos deemed it necessary to interrupt at that moment. 'I am afraid Miss Ashley does not have the time to talk with you any more right now, Miguel,' he said, causing the boy's lips to droop once more, and arousing a sense of indignation inside Christina.

She was about to protest when she saw Dom Carlos's eyes and the censure in them derived her of her resentment so that she coloured and thrust her hands awkwardly into her trousers' pockets.

Miguel caught his uncle's hand. 'Will—will Miss Ashley be able to come and talk with me again?' he asked appealingly.

Christina pressed her lips together, and Dom Carlos gave a faint smile. 'Maybe, Miguel, maybe,' he conceded, and with that the boy had to be content.

Christina said goodbye, aware of a curious lump in her throat as Miguel raised a thin pale hand in farewell. She looked impatiently at the man by her side and then walked quickly round the pool to where the open french doors of the lounge provided an escape from the boy's wistful stare.

'No, Miss Ashley, not there!' said Dom Carlos, as she reached the lounge doors. 'This way, please. My aunt is waiting to meet you.'

Christina felt unwilling to appease him. The indifferent way he had treated the boy's request to see her again was like a tangible thing between them, and she wanted to say that she had no desire to meet some aristocratic old woman when a boy, a gentle unassuming boy, was being forced to sit alone out there in the shadow of the gallery. She glanced back once as Dom Carlos indicated that she should precede him through an arched entrance into a cool panelled room and then turned her attention to her immediate surroundings.

Now they were in a less imposing apartment. She

supposed it could have been used as a study, there was a low desk under the window, but there were cabinets, too, containing a rare collection of ivory and jade, and the armchairs were too deep and comfortable for such a businesslike room.

A woman was seated in one of these armchairs, and she looked up curiously at their entrance, her eyes narrowing as they alighted on Christina's boyish appearance.

Christina stared at her in surprise. She had been expecting a woman in her sixties, but instead Dom Carlos's aunt could have been his contemporary. She was no more than forty, with immaculately sleek dark hair, dressed in the inevitable black, pearls about her slender throat. 'Carlos,' she said, and her voice was pleasantly accented, 'I saw you talking to Miguel. Is this the—young person you mentioned to me?'

Christina didn't like the way the other woman was regarding her, and when Dom Carlos put out a hand to draw her forward to be introduced, she resisted. But his hand at her wrist tightened almost cruelly, and she was forced to move forward against her will.

'*Sim*, Tia Inez, this is Miss Christina Ashley. Miss Ashley—this is my aunt, Donna Inez Valheiro.'

Christina took the hand Donna Inez extended politely, and said: 'How do you do, *senhora*?'

'I am quite well, thank you,' replied Inez Valheiro, inclining her head. 'You have spoken to Miss Ashley, Carlos?'

Carlos Ramirez shook his head. 'Not yet, Inez,' he replied.

Christina frowned. What was this? What had he to speak to her about? She was disturbed and intrigued, not least by the strange relationship between these two.

Her host walked to the cocktail cabinet. 'May I offer you some wine, Inez?' he suggested, changing the subject. 'And you, Miss Ashley?'

Christina glanced self-consciously at her casual attire. It seemed ridiculous to ask for sherry, but she did. Dom Carlos raised his eyebrows, but made no objections, and then he approached his aunt and handed her a glass of wine.

When they were all drinking, he said: 'Won't you sit down, Miss Ashley? I have a proposition to put to you.'

Christina subsided on to the edge of an armchair. She was loath to sit in his presence. It made the disadvantage she suffered greater. But as his aunt was seated she felt obliged to agree.

'Yes?' she said curiously.

'Yes.' Dom Carlos studied the wine in his glass critically, searching it for blemishes and apparently finding none from the satisfaction in his face. 'This wine, *menina*, was made from grapes grown in my vineyards.'

Christina sighed. 'The proposition, *senhor*,' she prompted, rather impatiently.

'Oh, yes, the proposition.' Dom Carlos lowered his glass. 'It is quite simple, *menina*. I want you to come here—to stay at the *quinta*—and be a companion to Miguel!'

CHAPTER FOUR

For several minutes there was complete silence in the room, and then Christina realised that it was up to her to make some remark. Donna Inez was sitting forward in her chair, her wine forgotten, her eyes intent on their young visitor, while Carlos Ramirez seemed, as usual, completely indifferent to whatever comment she might make. He had lit a cheroot and was inhaling deeply, his eyes fixed on some point beyond the environs of this room.

Christina sipped her sherry desperately, seeking words to express herself. 'But, *senhor*,' she began awkwardly, 'how could I stay at the *quinta*? I have to return to England in September.'

Carlos Ramirez lowered his disturbing gaze to hers. 'This is merely July, Miss Ashley. All we ask is three months of your time. And naturally you will be suitably recompensed for your services.'

Christina coloured. With this man she seemed constantly to be doing that, and it infuriated her. 'But I don't understand——' she began again.

'I agree. You do not.' Carlos Ramirez's voice was curt. 'Miguel needs the company of young people—perhaps only one young person, like himself. But it is not an easy situation. The children of our friends—our business associates—are like Miguel, well-behaved, subdued if you like. In Miguel's depressed state, this is not enough.'

Christina sighed. 'I'm not a child, *senhor*!' she stated flatly.

Dom Carlos raised his eyebrows. It was his only concession to the fact that she had spoken. 'We have tried everything to arouse an interest in life in the boy—companionship, travel, therapy.' He shrugged his broad shoulders, and she could see the muscles rippling beneath the fine, expensive material of his suit. 'Nothing succeeds. Miguel remains—withdrawn, obsessed with his own condition.'

'Won't you at least try to help us, Miss Ashley?' Donna Inez spoke now. 'You are—what would you say —our last resort?' She sighed. 'When Carlos discovered who you were, he had this possibly—crazy idea that you might be sufficiently—how shall I put it—different, diverting, to arouse a spark of interest in Miguel. The boy is ill, Miss Ashley. We are not unaware of that. But his illness is as much of the mind as of the body.'

Christina got jerkily to her feet. 'But I'm no psycho-analyst, *senhora*,' she protested.

'Miguel does not respond to psycho-analysis,' remarked Carlos Ramirez, his eyes penetratingly intent. 'He is indifferent—apathetic—emotionless. We need someone, or something, to break down this kind of mental barrier, but as I have said, nothing works. We are therefore obliged to seek solutions for ourselves, do you understand me, Miss Ashley?'

Christina spread her hands. 'But what makes you think I could be of any use?'

Carlos Ramirez stubbed out his cheroot in the base of a heavy onyx ash tray. 'I am not sure that you can, Miss Ashley. But I am prepared to try anything.'

Christina shook her head slowly. 'I think you've chosen the wrong person——' she began.

'On the contrary,' snapped Carlos Ramirez, and for the first time his eyes flashed with anger. 'On the contrary, you are the *only* person!'

'What do you mean?' Christina stared at him, perplexed.

'It is this very—*perversity* in you which might appeal to Miguel,' he said sharply. 'You are not like anyone he has ever encountered before. You say you are not a child! Very well then, behave like an adult and try to show Miguel that his life need not necessarily be the empty thing he imagines it to be.'

'*Carlos!*' Donna Inez sounded shocked, but Christina barely heard her protest.

Gripping her glass very tightly, she said: 'What you're really telling me, *senhor*, is that you would not allow me to associate with Miguel in the normal way, but because of his condition you're prepared to suffer dissension in place of indifference, is that it?'

Ramirez's face was grim and cold. 'I will disregard that remark, Miss Ashley,' he said tersely.

'Don't bother,' said Christina defiantly, trying to ignore the feeling of hurt bitterness inside her. 'I'm leaving. I'll find my own way back to the hotel——' And without attempting to apologise to Donna Inez, who was sitting, horrified at this exchange, she walked out of the room.

She heard Carlos Ramirez's quick-drawn breath, and the shocked ejaculation of his aunt, and then she was hurrying along the patio to the open french doors which she knew would lead her through to safety.

Miguel's chair had gone, she saw, and she wondered where for a brief moment before hard fingers closed round her wrist and she was brought up short to face Carlos Ramirez. She had not heard him behind her, the soles of his suede shoes making no sound, and besides, she had been too wrapped up in her own humiliation to imagine he might follow her. Surely that was forbidden for someone like him. Against his code of honour! To send Alfredo Seguin would have been much more in character.

67

'A moment, *menina!*' he said harshly. 'I have not given you permission to leave.'

Christina struggled to free herself. She was a little frightened now by the concentrated violence in those strange feline eyes of his, and she wondered belatedly whether her actions could in any way create difficulties for Bruce.

'I didn't know I needed permission to avoid being insulted,' she said, tremulously.

'I did not insult you!' he stated coldly.

'Didn't you?' Christina clenched her free hand.

'No, I did not.' Ramirez released her wrist abruptly, and she rubbed her reddened flesh painfully. 'I'm sorry if I've hurt you.'

Christina widened her eyes. 'Is that an apology?' she enquired, and then bent her head, realising she was inviting more violence.

For a moment she thought he might retaliate, and then he seemed to get himself in control, for he said with deliberate detachment: 'Well, Miss Ashley? Are you going to accept my proposition?'

Christina glanced along the patio and noticed Donna Inez standing watching them anxiously from the doorway of the room in which they had taken the wine. 'Isn't this a little unorthodox, *senhor?*' she suggested mockingly, unable to prevent the taunt. 'Oughtn't we to have a chaperon?'

'*Com a breca!*' he glared at her impatiently. 'You invite insult by your attitude! No, we do not need a chaperon at this moment. Answer my question—will you stay and help Miguel?'

Christina turned away, cupping her elbow in the palm of her other hand, supporting her chin with her knuckles. 'I don't see how I can. I've promised to help my brother and his wife at the hotel.'

Ramirez made an impatient sound. 'I have already spoken to your brother. He is agreeable.'

Christina's hands dropped to her sides. 'How dare you ask him without first consulting me?' she demanded hotly, turning to him.

'In my country one does not invite the child to the picnic without first consulting the parents, *menina*,' said Carlos Ramirez with all his cool composure that for a few moments Christina had succeeded in shifting.

'And is that what you think this is—a picnic?' she asked, angrily. 'Well, I'm sorry, *senhor*, but I'm going to have to disappoint you.' She sighed, remorse for the boy momentarily overwhelming her. She had liked Miguel, she felt compassion for him, she would have liked to have tried to help him, but the idea of living in close proximity with this man was unacceptable. 'I prefer the freedom I have at the hotel.'

Ramirez raised his eyes heavenward, and she could sense that he was controlling his temper with difficulty. 'You would have freedom here, *menina*, I promise you,' he said.

Christina shook her head, and Ramirez smote his fist into the palm of his other hand. She could tell he was fighting an inner battle with himself and she moved slowly towards the french doors.

But he turned as she reached them and there was a grim expression on his face. 'I do not wish to say this, *menina*,' he said heavily, 'but you are forcing my hand. Must I remind you that your brother's livelihood depends on the good will of the Ramirez corporation?'

Christina halted, staring at him. 'What do you mean?'

Ramirez spread a careless hand. 'Surely it is obvious. As I say, I have no wish to threaten anyone——'

'But you would!' Christina broke in. 'Of course, you're Bruce's landlord, aren't you? His *senhorio*!' Her cheeks burned. 'You must be very desperate, *senhor*!'

He lifted his shoulders in a defeated gesture. 'I am.'

Christina scuffed her toes irritably. 'So what you're actually saying is—help Miguel, or else!'

Ramirez raked a hand through the thickness of his dark hair and for a moment he was disturbingly honest. 'I love my nephew, *menina*,' he said quietly.

Christina heaved a sigh. 'And if I come here, you agree that I should have a free hand? You will not constantly be on my neck demanding the—*formalities* —which appear to mean so much to you?'

Ramirez straightened his shoulders. 'So far as I am concerned you need have no qualms on that score. As to my aunt——' He made an expressive gesture. 'No doubt she will object. But she will say nothing.' He brought out his case of cheroots. 'I am away a lot, visiting my vineyards, conducting my businesses. Miguel will be glad of your company if nothing else. And if anything else is achieved, then it is well.' He shrugged. 'Does that satisfy you?'

Christina bit her lip. 'I suppose it will have to, won't it?'

Ramirez's lips tightened. 'Don't make it too difficult for me, *menina*,' he said harshly. 'Freedom is one thing; arrogance is another!'

As you should know, thought Christina bitterly to herself.

Just at that moment a uniformed maid came to advise her master that lunch was served, and with a casual gesture Ramirez indicated that Christina should precede him into the building.

Lunch was served in a small dining room, small by *quinta* standards, that is, on a polished table, the patina of which must have been over a hundred years old. Ladderbacked chairs were stiff and formal, as was the conversation.

Although Donna Inez ate lunch with them, Miguel apparently ate elsewhere, and Christina was tempted to ask why. But she decided it would not do to ask too many questions straight away. Still, she consoled herself, as she swallowed some of the delicious chicken soup that the maidservant had provided, it might suit her purpose that Miguel ate alone. She could join him and thus avoid long discussions with Dom Carlos on what progress she was making.

The soup was followed by *presunto*, smoked ham, with fresh salad and potato croquettes, accompanied by some excellent white wine which Donna Inez complimented her nephew upon. But by the time the dessert stage was reached Christina had had enough and refused the sticky concoction of egg yolk and sugar which Inez Valheiro seemed to find so delectable. Dom Carlos ate very little, his expression brooding, and Christina was glad when the coffee stage was reached. Although it was strong and black she drank several cups, longing for the end of this uncomfortable meal.

At last it was over and they all rose and left the dining room. Donna Inez excused herself from them in the hall, and made her way upstairs, and Christina took the opportunity to make her own departure.

'You will return tomorrow,' Ramirez informed her inflexibly. 'I will send Seguin for you at ten o'clock.'

Christina knew there was no point in arguing with him, and she waited patiently while he summoned Alfredo to drive her back to the hotel.

Curiously though, when the time came for her to climb into the back of the huge black limousine, she felt reluctant to leave. Her eyes were drawn irresistibly to the tall dark man by her side, the pale line of his scar accentuated in the blaze of the afternoon sunlight.

He caught her eyes upon him and immediately his expression assumed its normal withdrawn appearance. 'Do not worry, *menina*,' he observed in an undertone. 'I shall not inflict my presence upon you more often than is absolutely necessary. I realise this ugliness offends you. I am sorry.'

Christina shook her head helplessly, and then Alfredo was opening the car door and she had perforce to get inside. But as the car moved down the drive, she looked back at the figure on the steps and there was an awful feeling of emptiness inside her.

Bruce and Sheila were in their sitting room when she returned and they looked at her almost accusingly as she entered the room.

'Well?' said Sheila irritably. 'What's going on?'

Christina lifted her shoulders. 'I thought you knew.'

Bruce rose to his feet. 'Dom Carlos said he wanted you to go to the *quinta*—to be companion to his nephew or something. Is that right?'

Christina nodded. 'Yes. Miguel.'

Bruce shook his head. 'But why? Why you? Are you going to do it?'

'Yes.' Christina flung herself into a chair.

'And what about us, that's what I'd like to know!' exclaimed Sheila shrilly. 'I suppose you didn't think about us, did you? Bruce invited you out here to help us—not some kid whose parents must be positively rolling in cash!'

'It's not like that,' Christina sighed. 'The boy's an invalid, confined to a wheelchair.'

'But you're not a nurse, Chris!' exclaimed Bruce impatiently.

'It's not a nurse Miguel needs,' replied Christina, frowning. 'He's—well—introversive. He's lost interest in the usual things that would interest any normal boy.'

'Oh, really!' Sheila was scornful. 'And you're going to change all that, I suppose.'

'I doubt it,' responded Christina honestly. 'But his uncle wants me to try—and I agreed.'

Bruce moved restlessly about the room. 'You realise

72

if you fail that it will reflect on us—all of us?' he said.

Christina bit her lip. 'Then let's hope I don't, shall we?' she suggested, quietly.

Sheila rose now. 'Well, I think it's an absolute cheek! Coming here on the pretext of helping Bruce, and then clearing off at the first opportunity!' She pursed her lips. 'Are you going to permit this, Bruce?'

Bruce shrugged his shoulders. 'I don't see how I can prevent her if she has decided to go,' he answered wearily. 'Do you really want to do this, Chris? I shouldn't have thought it was your style.'

'Of course it's her style!' Sheila's lip curled. 'Who would turn down the chance to live in luxury at the Quinta Ramirez? Christina's no fool, whatever else she might be!'

'I've told you—it's not like that!' Christina flared indignantly. She was tempted to tell Sheila exactly what Dom Carlos had said, but she knew if she did so, Bruce would get on his high horse and refuse to allow her to go, and therefore jeopardise his own livelihood. And she couldn't allow that.

Sheila lit a cigarette. 'When do you leave?'

'Tomorrow. Dom Carlos is sending the car for me at ten o'clock.'

Bruce looked at his sister reproachfully. 'I thought you liked it here. I thought you enjoyed helping about the hotel.'

'I did—I do!' Christina sighed. 'But what would you do, faced with such a decision? The boy's ill, I've told you. Withdrawn, apathetic, if you like. Lonely! Maybe I can shake him out of it. Dom Carlos thinks it's worth a try. They've tried everything else.'

'But why you?' Sheila stared at her resentfully.

Christina bent her head, examining the ovals of her nails minutely. 'Because Dom Carlos considers me a prime example of emancipated youth, I suppose. At any rate, he realises my upbringing has been vastly

73

different from Miguel's.'

Sheila shook her head. 'Well, I think it's all highly suspect. Are you sure you've never met Dom Carlos before today?'

Christina controlled her colour by an immense effort of will. 'How could I?' she demanded, and Sheila had to admit defeat.

Even so, when Bruce came to her room that evening as she was packing her things, it took a great deal of determination to prevent her from pouring out the whole story to him from the moment she first encountered Dom Carlos on the beach two days ago. Bruce was naturally hurt at her decision to leave them, and it did not seem to occur to him to wonder whether his sister might have been coerced into accepting Dom Carlos's proposition.

The next morning, Christina was awake almost as soon as it was light, and as her clothes were already packed, she washed, put on her swimsuit and a smock and went downstairs soon after six.

She encountered Julio in the hall, but his eyes were guarded. 'I hear you are leaving us,' he said. 'To go and stay at the *quinta!*'

'That's right.' Christina was abrupt. She had no desire to have to explain her actions to Julio.

Julio shrugged. 'It is your business, of course——'

'Yes, it is.' Christina would have passed him, but he stopped her, stepping into her path.

'Where are you going?'

Christina sighed. 'To swim, if you must know.'

'May I come with you?'

Christina hesitated, and then relented. Why not? Julio had nothing to do with her predicament. 'All right,' she agreed. 'Are you ready now?'

Julio half smiled. 'Of course.'

'What about—well—the chores you have to do?'

Julio moved towards the open doorway. 'I will work

74

especially hard when I get back,' he promised laughingly.

It was after seven by the time they got back. It had been marvellous in the water at that hour and Christina had delayed the moment when they must return to the hotel. Julio was good company and she didn't know when next she would be allowed such freedom.

Sheila was not at all pleased when she encountered them on their return. Her eyes flashed fire at Julio before turning contemptuously to Christina.

'You realise you're inviting gossip by behaving so irresponsibly, Christina!' she snapped coldly.

'There was no harm,' exclaimed Julio impatiently.

'Of course there wasn't,' confirmed Christina, sick of Sheila's constant dissension. 'For heaven's sake, Sheila, we weren't alone! There were several people on the beach!'

Sheila sniffed. 'Well, I can only say I'm glad someone else is going to be responsible for your actions from now on,' she retorted. 'I can't imagine Dom Carlos allowing you this kind of licence!'

Christina opened her mouth to make some retort and then closed it again. She would not argue with Sheila, she *must* not. Who knew when she got angry what she might not say, and she had no intention of ruining everything now.

Without making any reply, she said goodbye to Julio and went up the stairs to her room.

'Your duties here aren't over yet, madam!' Sheila called angrily after her, disappointed that Christina wasn't rising to the bait.

Christina made no reply, and when she came downstairs half an hour later, bathed and dressed, her damp hair secured as usual with the elastic band, Sheila was nowhere to be seen.

Christina ate breakfast in the kitchen with Maria,

and then Bruce appeared. 'Ready for off?' he enquired gruffly.

Christina nodded. 'I'm sorry, Bruce.'

'Oh, that's okay.'

'And in any case, I'm only going to be a few miles away. I'll come and see you—often.'

'Will you?' Bruce looked sceptical. Then he sighed. 'But whatever happens, you know if you run into difficulties—I mean I don't know what kind of difficulties you're likely to run into at the *quinta*—but if you do meet any trouble, you know where to come.'

'Oh, Bruce!' Christina sprang up and hugged him. 'Darling Bruce, I wish—I wish I'd never said I would go!'

Bruce shook his head, holding her at arm's length. 'Don't be silly, honey. It's probably a great opportunity for you. After all, history's your subject, and the *quinta* is a relic of a bygone era, isn't it? You'll be able to examine it in detail, and they've probably got a library which will drive you into raptures!'

Christina looked alert. 'Do you think so?' she exclaimed, the details of her proposed occupation not really meaning much to her yet.

'Sure!' Bruce frowned. 'And they can't expect you to be nursemaid to this boy all the time. How old is he?'

'Didn't Dom Carlos tell you?'

'No, I guess not.' Bruce shook his head. 'He may have done, I suppose, but I was too shocked to take it all in.'

Christina bit her lip. 'Well, I should say he's about thirteen or fourteen.'

'And where are his parents?'

'I don't know.' Christina made a helpless gesture. 'I don't know much at all. Just that Miguel is a lonely child, and needs companionship.'

'I should have thought someone of his own age would have provided a more suitable companion,' remarked Bruce dryly.

Christina tucked a strand of hair behind her ear. 'Maybe,' she conceded awkwardly.

'Well, watch what you're doing,' Bruce said at last. 'Don't let them bully you!'

Christina chuckled. 'Can you see that?'

'Not actually, no. But there's a first time for everything.' Bruce hesitated a moment. 'Tell me something, Chris! What's your opinion of Dom Carlos?'

Christina wet her suddenly dry lips. 'He's very—well —formal, isn't he?'

'Is that all?'

'What do you want me to say, Bruce?'

Bruce hunched his shoulders. 'I hear from Maria that he once had quite a reputation with women. That was before he was scarred, of course.'

'I see.' Christina looked thoughtful. 'How did it—I mean—do you know how he was scarred?'

'In a plane crash, I believe. Maria didn't seem too certain of the details.'

Christina nodded. 'Oh!'

Bruce heaved a sigh. 'Well, like I said, if anything— bothers you——'

'Oh, Bruce, really!' Christina managed a smile. 'Believe me, you need have no qualms on that score. There's a perfectly adequate chaperon in the person of Donna Inez Valheiro, his aunt, and besides——' she laughed suddenly—'to him I'm just a child! Yes, it's true. Mentally, I'm sure, he classes me with Miguel.'

'Then perhaps it's just as well,' said Bruce heavily. 'Besides, he's old enough to be your father.'

'I suppose he is.' Christina bent her head. 'What time is it?'

'Just after nine. What time did Ramirez say he would send for you?'

'Ten o'clock.' Christina compressed her lips. 'I suppose I ought to be bringing my suitcase downstairs.'

'I'll get it.' Bruce walked to the door. 'And Christina?'

'Yes.'

'You won't forget what I've said—about anything?'

Christina shook her head gently, and Bruce went out.

The black Mercedes drew to a halt outside the Hotel Inglês at precisely one minute to ten o'clock. Christina was in the hall with Bruce, and Sheila appeared when she heard the car. To Christina's surprise she had changed into a smart two-piece, and her expression when she saw Alfredo Seguin was positively fulsome. She invited him in to take coffee, but the chauffeur politely refused.

'My orders are to take the *senhorita* straight back to the *quinta*,' he apologised with great charm. 'Are you ready, *senhorita*?'

'Yes.' Christina looked at her brother. 'Goodbye, Bruce.'

'*Ate logo*, Chris.'

Bruce kissed her warmly and then Sheila moved forward and did likewise. After what she had said this morning, Christina felt like drawing back from that artificial embrace, but for Bruce's sake she steeled herself to accept it.

Then she was free and Alfredo was helping her into the back of the limousine. Her suitcase and holdall were stowed in the capacious boot, and then they were off.

The drive to the *quinta* seemed to be accomplished much quicker than before. In no time at all, it seemed, the lodge-keeper was opening the heavy iron gates with their scrolled embellishments to allow them through, and then they were moving swiftly up the drive to the house itself.

Donna Inez met her on the steps of the building, and gave a faint smile as Christina climbed out. This morning Christina was wearing a short red pleated skirt and a white shirt blouse, and not even Donna Inez could fault her clothes.

'*Bom dia*, Miss Ashley,' she said politely. 'Come inside, won't you? Alfredo will see to your luggage. Juana knows which room you are to occupy and will see that your things are taken there and unpacked.'

Christina hesitated. 'Juana?' she queried.

'*Sim*, Juana.' Donna Inez indicated that Christina should accompany her up the steps. 'Juana is my nephew's housekeeper, *menina*. You will come to know all the members of the household eventually.'

'Yes.' Christina was polite, and they entered the cool tiled hall of the *quinta*.

'We will have coffee,' went on Donna Inez, in much the same inflexible way as Dom Carlos gave his commands. 'Then one of the maids will show you your room.'

Christina was about to speak, but her hostess moved across the hall and into a light modern lounge that opened from it, and she had perforce to follow her. The high ceiling of the room was intricately carved and the walls were panelled in a pale wood which gave a perfect background for a collection of flower prints which Christina found quite fascinating. Donna Inez, when questioned, explained rather indifferently that they had been done almost a hundred years ago by an artist friend of Dom Carlos's grandfather. To Christina, to whom such beauty was not an everyday accompaniment to living, Donna Inez's attitude was alien.

Coffee must have been ordered before the arrival of the car, for now a uniformed maid brought in the tray containing the heavy silver service, and she cast a speculative glance in Christina's direction.

Christina came to a chair when Donna Inez insisted, and then said: 'When may I see Miguel?'

Donna Inez looked up from pouring the coffee.

'Miguel works with his professor in the morning. And after lunch, he rests for an hour. You may see him after his rest.'

Christina sipped her coffee frowningly. 'He wasn't working when I came yesterday morning,' she pointed out.

Donna Inez regarded her a little irritably. 'His lessons were over for the morning, Miss Ashley. Senhor Perez sometimes allows him half an hour outside before lunch.'

Christina replaced her cup in its saucer. 'Senhor Perez is his professor?'

'Of course.'

'Of course.' Christina bit her lip, refusing one of the delicate biscuits Donna Inez offered. 'Don't you think, while I am here at least, it would be a good idea if Miguel only worked for a couple of hours in the morning, *senhora*?'

Donna Inez's lips tightened. 'I do not make decisions regarding my nephew's charge,' she replied, rather stiffly. 'You will have to take the matter up with him.'

Christina shrugged and lifted her coffee cup again. If Miguel worked all morning and slept half the afternoon, what was she supposed to do in the meantime?

She wondered suddenly whether Dom Carlos was in the *quinta*. Was he here, or was he out, about his business?

Donna Inez looked at her intently. 'I should tell you, Miss Ashley,' she said. 'While I have agreed with my nephew that you should be given this opportunity to work with Miguel, I cannot approve. Miguel was never an extrovert. He was always a quiet, thinking child. His illness may have much to do with his depression, and then again it may not.'

Christina finished her coffee suddenly and rose to her feet. She had no intention of entering into a discussion with Donna Inez concerning her own merits in this. She had enough doubts of her ability to be successful as it was without Dom Carlos's aunt adding to them.

'May I see my room, *senhora*?' she requested politely, and Donna Inez clicked her tongue, and stood up.

'Very well, Miss Ashley. I will arrange it,' she responded curtly.

Christina's luggage had been taken to her apartments which proved to be far more luxurious than she had even imagined. Her rooms were on the first floor, at the back of the house, overlooking the azure blue of the swimming pool. French doors opened on to the encircling gallery and it was possible to walk round and descend to the ground floor by means of a grilled stairway. This meant that she did not have to enter the main building until she wished to do so to reach her room.

But it was the rooms themselves which enchanted her. She had been given a sitting room, bedroom and bathroom for her own use, all opening out of one another. The bedroom was enormous, although the furnishings were surprisingly modern. A long fitted wardrobe with louvre doors dwarfed her small collection of garments which had already been unpacked, while the bed was wide enough to accommodate half a dozen adults comfortably. The carpet underfoot was white and fluffy, and she took off her sandals and allowed her toes to curl in the pile.

The fittings in her sitting room were less aggressively modern. The tapestry-covered wing chairs which stood beside an attractive pink marble fireplace were obviously faded, but their cushioned seats were exceptionally comfortable. There was a desk, which she felt sure was an antique, and a standard lamp beside it with an exquisitely carved stem. More up to date were the bookshelves which were filled with literature of all kinds, including some English novels, and there was an electric kettle and a hotplate in one corner to enable her to make tea for herself if she so desired.

But it was the bathroom which gave her the most pleasure. Larger than any bathroom she had ever seen, it was tiled in green and white mosaic tiles, with a step-in bath with gold taps. Glass shelves round the walls were filled with a variety of bath salts and essences, cleansing creams and liquids, and talcs, and she felt sure she would never use half of them. Huge, fleecy towels were hung on heated rails while there were mirrors everywhere.

She paused a moment to wonder whether Carlos Ramirez had a bathroom like this, and then squashed the thought. With his intense awareness of his appearance, however unfounded, he would never allow himself to be seen from so many angles.

Out on the gallery, she looked down into the lucid waters of the pool, wondering if anyone ever despoiled its undisturbed depths. What manner of illness was Miguel's, that he must spend his days in a wheelchair, always a spectator and never a participant? She wondered whether he had ever tried swimming, whether if his legs would not respond to anything else, they would respond to the therapy of water. She shrugged. No doubt if it had already been tried it had failed.

With a sigh, she turned and went back into her sitting room, wandering about restlessly. Where was Ramirez? Why couldn't he have been here to meet her so that she could have voiced her opinions to him right away? As it was she was left to kick her heels for the best part of three hours with only lunch with Donna Inez to look forward to.

CHAPTER FIVE

IN fact, lunch was brought to her room, and Christina ate her lonely meal without enjoyment. It wasn't that she particularly desired the company of Donna Inez, but it annoyed her that somewhere in this mausoleum Miguel would be eating his lunch, too, and they could have had the meal together.

After lunch, a knock signalled the arrival of the maid to take away the tray, and Christina stopped her as she would have left again.

'Where does Miguel eat his lunch?' she asked. 'Could you tell me where his room is?'

The maid frowned. 'The *menino* will be resting now, *senhorita*,' she replied.

Christina stiffened her shoulders. 'I realise that. I just wondered where his room was, that's all.'

The maid looked doubtful. 'Perhaps if you asked Donna Inez—or Dom Carlos——' she began cautiously.

Christina grew impatient. 'For heaven's sake,' she said, 'I only want to know where his room is. I'm here to be company for him, after all.'

The maid hesitated. 'But Dom Carlos is away today, *senhorita*.'

'I don't want to see Dom Carlos!' retorted Christina, heatedly. 'Don't worry. I shan't involve you in anything.'

The maid sighed. 'I can indicate his room, *senhorita*,' she conceded at last.

'That's all I want you to do,' retorted Christina, with feeling.

She followed the maid along the panelled corridor which led back to the gallery above the main hall, and Christina took time to observe the portraits which lined the corridor. They were all of black-browed men, and sallow-faced women, dressed in various modes of fashion common to the eighteenth and nineteenth centuries. Their children, who in some instances were clustered round their feet, or perched precariously on their parents' laps looked many, but subdued and unreal, scarcely virile enough to survive the rigours of life at that time. Christina was amazed that any one of them should have been strong enough to sustain the Ramirez line, but then maybe she was being unkind, or perhaps the artists, whoever they were, preferred the delicacy of feature that was so evident.

At the head of the baroque staircase, the maid halted and pointed down the corridor which began at the opposite side of the gallery.

'The rooms you seek are down there, *senhorita,*' she said, with obvious reluctance. 'Now, may I go?'

Christina sighed. 'I suppose so. Thank you.'

'*Sim, senhorita.*'

The maid hastened down the stairs with the tray and disappeared along the corridor which apparently led to the kitchens. Christina leaned over the rail and watched her until she was out of sight.

Then she crossed the gallery and hesitated at the arched entrance to that other part of the building. There were several doors opening on to the corridor. How could she possibly tell which was Miguel's? And even if the maid had pointed out the actual door, what could she do?

As she stood there however, the problem was resolved for her. A panelled door a few yards down the corridor opened and a small, dapper little man with a moustache and beard appeared, and then stared incredulously at Christina.

'*Senhorita?*' he challenged abruptly.

Christina sighed. 'You must be—Senhor Perez,' she ventured, taking a chance.

The little man closed the door behind him, and as he did so, Christina heard the sound of Miguel calling to him. It had to be Miguel. There was such a note of unreasonable despair in that youthful voice.

Christina took a step forward, but Senhor Perez approached quickly and she was forced to step back a pace. 'Senhorita—Ashley, is it not?' he queried, his accent only slightly pronounced.

'That's right.' Christina heard the plaintive voice again. 'Isn't that Miguel calling you?'

Senhor Perez's eyes narrowed. 'It is the time for his rest, *senhorita*. I am afraid Miguel does not take kindly to discipline.'

Christina was astounded. It sounded so unlike the Miguel she had encountered that she almost gasped. 'Well, as he is awake, *senhor*, may I see him?'

Senhor Perez shook his head. 'I regret, not yet, *senhorita*. Dom Carlos would not wish him to be disturbed at this time.'

Christina told herself she was being unnecessarily demanding, and possibly turning Senhor Perez into an antagonist, but she was determined to see the boy. There had been something in that plaintive call which had twisted her heart and remembering his lonely vigil by the pool she refused to be put off.

'Dom Carlos has given me permission to deal as I think fit with Miguel,' she stated, with assumed bravado. 'And if he objects, no doubt he will make his objections to me!'

Senhor Perez frowned. 'Donna Inez has explained that you are to have the boy's time after his afternoon rest. I must insist you adhere to these arrangements.'

Christina looked impatient. 'These arrangements were made without my knowledge or consent, *senhor*,' she retorted calmly. 'Miguel and I will make our own arrangements!'

Senhor Perez looked furious. 'You are insolent, *senhorita!*'

'On the contrary, I am trying to accomplish what I was brought here to accomplish, *senhor*. And now, if you'll excuse me ...'

Before he could stop her she had walked past him down the corridor, halting before the door of the room she had seen him close moments before. She knocked, and then ignoring the professor's angry glare, she entered the room.

The room was light and attractive, decorated very much with a boy in mind, overlooking the courtyard and fountain in front of the *quinta*. And from here, Christina could see the sea, sparkling and iridescent in the distance.

Then her eyes went to the figure lying inert in the middle of the enormous bed, the sheets secured tightly across his thin young body. His eyes lit up when he saw her, and he struggled up on to his pillows, disturbing the rigidly smooth coverlet. Christina approached the bed and smiled.

'Hello, Miguel.'

'You've come,' he said, shaking his head. 'My uncle said you might. I did not believe him.'

Christina perched on the end of the bed. 'Why not?'

'I didn't think you would want to come here. Everything is so—so—dull! I thought you would say no.'

Christina felt a twinge of remorse. She had said no.

'Well, I'm here now,' she remarked warmly. 'And we're going to make sure life isn't so dull from now on.'

Miguel glanced suddenly towards the door. 'Did—did Perez see you come in here?' he asked urgently.

Christine frowned. 'Yes, of course. Why?'

Miguel sank back on his pillows. 'He won't allow

you to stay here. I'm to rest, you see. I'm not allowed visitors at this time.'

Christina chuckled, and Miguel stared at her in amazement. 'Your Senhor Perez didn't "allow" me to come. I just came. Your uncle has given me a free hand where you're concerned, and so long as I don't do anything stupid like wearing you out or anything like that, I guess he won't make too many objections.'

Miguel's eyes sparkled. 'You really told Perez that?'

'More or less.' Christina slid off the bed and wandered curiously round the room. 'This is a nice room, isn't it? I guess you know that.' She lifted a scale model of a powerful diesel engine from an intricate layout that had been installed on a table in one corner of the room. The table was at a height that made it easy for Miguel to use the layout from his wheelchair. 'This is magnificent, isn't it?' She turned to look at him. 'What are your interests? Did you make these collections?' She indicated a series of mounted butterflies that hung on the wall beside some plastic-protected sheets of stamps.

The animation in Miguel's face died as suddenly as it had appeared. 'I don't do much in that direction, *senhorita*,' he replied reluctantly. 'My uncle bought all these things. They do not interest me. I read, of course, but that is all.'

Christina bit her lip. She must try not to rush things. That would never do. She had to win Miguel's confidence gradually, teach him that nothing was ever impossible if one was determined enough.

She replaced the diesel carefully on its rails and came back to the bed, looking down at him intently. Apart from the pallor of his cheeks, he was a remarkably attractive boy, and in a few years' time she could imagine him being as successful with the opposite sex as his uncle was reputed to have been. But only if something could be done now.

'How old are you, Miguel?' she asked.

Miguel pushed back a lock of dark hair which fell across his eyes. 'I am fifteen years of age,' he said carefully.

Christina was surprised. She had not realised he was as old as that. She sat on the side of his bed and took one of his hands. 'Tell me something,' she said gently. 'Did you really want me to come here? Are you glad I came?'

Miguel allowed his fingers to curl round hers. 'But yes,' he said, nodding. 'I am very glad.' Then he sighed. 'Do I have to stay in bed now? Couldn't I get up? We—we might sit beside the pool and talk.'

Christina hesitated. 'I don't see why not, if you're not tired,' she agreed cautiously.

Miguel struggled eagerly into a sitting position. Certainly he had moments when he forced movement into his body, but how long would it last once he got used to having her around?

Then he surprised her again by reaching out a hand and touching the thick swathe of hair which fell just below her shoulders. 'Is this real?' he asked wonderingly, fingering the golden strands.

Christina laughed softly. 'Well, it's not a wig, if that's what you mean,' she answered.

Miguel smiled. He had even white teeth and she thought he ought to smile more often. 'You know I didn't mean that,' he exclaimed.

Christina nodded. 'No, I know. And yes, it's natural.'

'But do you have to have it so?' Miguel indicated the securing elastic band. 'I liked it the other day when it was loose.'

Christina wrinkled her nose at him. 'All right. I'll loosen it.'

She tugged off the securing band and it immediately fell about her shoulders in a silken curtain.

Miguel was delighted. 'That is much better, Miss

Ashley,' he declared.

'My name is Christina,' she said firmly. 'Please use it.'

Miguel stared at her. 'May I?'

'Of course. Why not? A name is just a name.'

'All right—Christina!' His eyes sparkled brilliantly again, and he thrust both his hands into hers, linking their fingers. 'I—feel so excited! Almost as though something—unforeseen was about to happen!'

Christina touched his cheek gently. The wrists protruding from the sleeves of his pyjama jacket were painfully thin, and where the buttons of his jacket were unfastened at his neck she could see the bones of his shoulders. She had an almost overpowering impulse to gather him into her arms and hug him, but she suppressed it and he raised one of her hands to his lips.

It was a gallant gesture, typical of his race and breeding, and Christina bent towards him to kiss his cheek.

'*Miss Ashley!* Exactly what is going on here?'

The cold clipped tones were disturbingly familiar, and Christina's first impulse was to scramble off the bed and confront her employer on trembling legs. But she knew to do so would prove to Miguel, conclusively, that she was as much in awe of his uncle as he was. So she turned casually, and met his angry glare with challenging indifference.

Miguel's young face had suffused with colour, and he disentangled his hands from Christina's hurriedly, and said: 'Tio Carlos! Tia Inez said you were to be away all day!'

Carlos Ramirez advanced into the room, followed at a discreet distance by Senhor Perez. Christina rose now and as she did so she thought rather cynically that Miguel had been right in his premonition that something unforeseen was about to happen.

Carlos Ramirez's eyes fixed themselves upon her although he spared a moment to glance appraisingly at his nephew before saying: 'I repeat, *menina*, what is going on here?'

Christina stood, feet apart, her hands resting casually on her hips. 'Nothing untoward, *senhor*,' she responded calmly. 'Miguel and I were getting to know one another, that's all.'

Carlos Ramirez glanced round at Senhor Perez. 'But this is the time for Miguel's rest,' he stated curtly, returning his attention to her. 'Did not Senhor Perez inform you of this fact?'

Christina shrugged her slim shoulders. 'Senhor Perez informed me, yes. But as you can see, Miguel is wide awake, and by no means tired, and I see absolutely no reason why he should be forced to rest if he doesn't wish to do so.'

Senhor Perez's indrawn breath was hissingly audible, and Dom Carlos's eyes narrowed. 'Miss Ashley! When I invited you here to be a companion for Miguel, I did not give you permission to interfere with his daily routine——'

'Well, I should have thought that routine was the last thing Miguel needed!' interrupted Christina forcefully.

Dom Carlos tightened his lips. 'Miguel is not a well boy, *menina*. He needs this rest in the middle of the day. The *medicos* tell me so.'

'The same—*medicos*—no doubt, who have been unable to cure Miguel!' snapped Christina, throwing caution to the winds, annoyed that Ramirez should attempt to remonstrate with her here in front of Senhor Perez and the boy.

The tall Portuguese stared at her for a long moment and Christina was sure he would have liked to have used actual physical violence against her, so angry did he look. Then he seemed to control himself for he took a deep breath and said icily:

'I do not propose to argue with you here, Miss Ashley. We will go to my study.'

Miguel expelled his breath jerkily. 'Tio Carlos...' he began anxiously.

Ramirez turned to look at him and a little of the ice went out of his gaze. '*Sim*, Miguel?'

Miguel swallowed hard. 'You—you will not send— Miss Ashley away?'

Ramirez's jaw tightened. 'Rest now, Miguel,' he said, without expression.

Christina looked helplessly at the boy. He sank back against his pillows and there was a look of despair in his eyes. Angrily she turned back to her employer.

'Can't you give him an answer, *senhor*?' she demanded, and Senhor Perez gasped.

Ramirez had been walking towards the door, but now he halted and turned to look at her in amazement. 'There are limits to which I will permit you to go, *menina*, and you have reached them!' he bit out grimly.

Christina clenched her fists. 'Then look at your nephew, *senhor*! If you think my motives for inviting your anger are irresponsible, then consider what you're doing to *him*!'

Ramirez looked as though he would have liked to have ordered her out of the *quinta* then and there, but something, some inner dignity, forced him to dismiss the notion and look instead at Miguel. As before his expression softened as he looked at his nephew, and with an effort he forced a normal note into his voice.

'Do not alarm yourself, Miguel. I am sure this—controversy—with Miss Ashley can be ironed out quite satisfactorily. No doubt you will see her later—after your rest.'

Miguel propped himself up again. 'You promise, Tio Carlos?'

Ramirez's eyes narrowed. '*Sim*, Miguel. You have my word,' he replied curtly, and without another word he turned and walked out of the room.

Christina heaved a deep sigh and turned to look at Miguel before moving slowly towards the door. She closed one eye deliberately and was gratified to see Miguel's strained young face lighten slightly. And then she squared her shoulders and walked out into the corridor, closing the door behind her. No doubt Senhor Perez would take the greatest delight in settling his charge down again for his rest.

Dom Carlos waited some distance down the corridor and Christina couldn't entirely dismiss the feathering of apprehension that touched her spine. She had taken unnecessarily reckless liberties in defying Ramirez in this way and yet she knew that to succeed here she must not allow him to dominate her. She tried to avoid looking at his withdrawn countenance and when he said: 'Come!' in cold commanding tones she quickened her step and followed him obediently down the corridor.

They descended the stairs, Ramirez leading the way across the tiled hall below to where a lower corridor ran parallel with the front terrace of the *quinta*. They followed this corridor only a short distance however before he halted before double panelled doors and throwing one open he indicated that she should precede him into the room.

Christina averted her gaze as she passed him but then interest in her surroundings banished her apprehension.

Dom Carlos's study was quite a large room, the walls lined with books and cabinets, while a typewriter and several telephones stood on a table in one corner. The ceiling was high and arched like other ceilings in the *quinta*, and there were plum-coloured drapes at the tall windows. Skin rugs were strewn about the polished wood floor, and the only concession to comfort was a pair of deep leather armchairs situated at either side of the enormous mahogany desk which dominated the room. Dom Carlos closed the door behind them, and came round to stand at the far side of the desk, indicating that Christina should seat herself in the armchair opposite.

Christina reluctantly complied, and waited for Dom Carlos to do likewise, but instead he remained standing, regarding her with brooding appraisal.

Finally he said: 'What exactly was your intention in defying Perez like that?' It was obvious from the abruptness of the question that he was still having difficulty in controlling his temper and Christina wondered what he was really thinking.

She sighed. 'I wanted to see Miguel, *senhor*. Surely that's not so unreasonable? I understood my reasons for being brought here were to try and shake him out of this apathy he suffers. How am I supposed to do that if to all intents and purposes everything is to go on as before——'

'*Miss Ashley!*' He halted her outburst with an abrupt exclamation, and then leaned forward, the tips of his fingers resting on the leather surface of his desk. 'You have a saying in your country, do you not, that one should not attempt to run before one can walk?'

Christina made an indifferent movement of her shoulders. 'We have lots of sayings, *senhor*. One can always find one to fit the purpose. Besides, where was the harm? Miguel was not tired, and your Senhor Perez ignored Miguel when he called to him after he'd left Miguel's bedroom.'

Ramirez straightened. 'Miguel does not know the details of his condition, *menina*,' he said curtly. 'One cannot always permit an invalid to know what is best for him.'

'Oh, really!' Christina lay back in her chair resignedly. '*Senhor!* You brought me here on the pretext of being free to deal as I liked with Miguel——'

'*Bastante!*' he snapped, a muscle jerking in his jaw, but Christina got to her feet then.

'Let me finish!' she exclaimed. 'How am I supposed to win Miguel's confidence if you undermine my efforts at the outset?'

Ramirez stood very still for several moments after she had finished and then with controlled movements he reached for a cigar from a heavy carved wooden box on his desk and lit it with a gold lighter before speaking. Exhaling smoke into the tense atmosphere about them, he regarded her with disturbing intensity.

'Perhaps it would be better if you discussed Miguel a little less emotionally, *menina*,' he said at last. 'Sit down, and I will endeavour to explain a little of Miguel's medical history.'

Christina hesitated and then with a sigh she sank back into her chair. She had the distinct impression that she had been mentally throwing herself against a brick wall and it was not a pleasing experience. Just as she seemed to be making headway, Ramirez succeeded in changing the subject so adroitly that she was left feeling decidedly foolish.

Now he strolled to the tall windows looking out on to the sparkling waters of the fountain, smoking his cigar with calm indifference. Then he turned and surveyed her with composed deliberation.

'Miguel's—accident—occurred some three years ago. At the time, his injuries—this paralysis—was thought to be caused by pressure on the spine. But although Miguel has had several operations no conceivable improvement has been achieved, and it becomes apparent that there is no actual physical damage. That is not to say that Miguel could walk tomorrow—on the contrary, it would be most unlikely that he should. But it does mean that given time—and therapy—and the desire to do so, he could learn to use his limbs again.'

Christina frowned. 'But why shouldn't a boy of his age and opportunities want to walk again?'

Ramirez sighed and looked down at the glowing tip of his cigar. 'Who knows, *menina?*' He shrugged. 'There could be many reasons. Perhaps the fact that his parents were killed at the time of the accident is the most likely, though.'

Christina's lips parted and she leaned forward in her chair. 'His parents, *senhor?* That would be your brother and his wife?'

'No. My sister Teresa, and Raoul, her husband.' Ramirez came to the desk to stub out his cigar in the ashtray. 'They were killed in a plane crash, *menina.* Miguel and I were the sole survivors.'

Christina bent her head. 'I see.'

Ramirez straightened his broad shoulders. 'So? And now you have the facts, *menina.* But what you are not aware of are the day-to-day details of Miguel's existence. He eats little. He has no energy. He catches colds easily. In other words, he is a delicate child, and therefore must be treated with care.'

Christina looked up at him quickly. 'Has it occurred to you, *senhor*, that anyone who spends their days in a wheelchair, never exercising their bodies, only their minds, never has the opportunity to acquire an appetite or resilience against disease?'

Ramirez pressed his lips together grimly, pressing his balled fist into the palm of his hand. 'Miss Ashley! Do you imagine we have not tried to encourage Miguel to take some exercise? To use the facilities here at the *quinta* to expedite his recovery?' He took a deep breath. 'Of course we have! But it is no use!

95

Miguel refuses to behave like a normal human being. And he is an adept at making one feel that one is being unnecessarily harsh with him. If he is content to sit by the pool all day and read, or work at his studies with Senhor Perez, what can I do? Short of forcing my opinions on him, of course.'

Christina got to her feet again. 'But don't you see, if I'm to achieve anything at all, I must be allowed to go my own way?'

'I cannot permit you to run the risk of injuring Miguel's health!' Ramirez's eyes were bleak.

Christina lifted the heavy weight of her hair off her neck in an unconsciously provocative gesture, and Ramirez turned away, moving towards the windows again, thrusting his hands deep into the pockets of his immaculately creased trousers.

'Would you then allow Miguel a holiday, *senhor*?' she queried.

Ramirez turned, frowning. 'A holiday, *menina*? What do you mean?'

Christina shrugged. 'At the moment, I am told that Miguel works with Senhor Perez in the mornings, and rests for an hour after lunch. That means that my time with him will be limited to the late afternoon and early evening, doesn't it?'

'So?'

'So that's not enough!' she burst out. 'Look, Miguel is an intelligent boy. Surely he could be allowed to forgo lessons for a few weeks. Don't you have holidays here?'

'Of course.' Ramirez was remote. He seemed to be considering what she had said. 'Naturally as Miguel only has lessons in the morning he does not cover the curricula common to most schools. Consequently his holidays are of a shorter duration.'

Christina shook her head. 'Surely you can see that it would be better if we could be together in the morn-

96

ings. I can drive. Perhaps we could go on outings together.'

'You go too quickly for me, *menina*.' Ramirez tapped his fingers against the leather surface of his desk. 'Should you desire to take Miguel driving, I will put Seguin at your convenience.'

Christina heaved a sigh. 'Why? Don't you trust me? Don't you consider me an adequate driver?'

Ramirez's eyes narrowed. 'I will consider the matter of the schooling, *menina*,' he said, and Christina scuffed her toe against a rug resentfully.

'Can I go now?' she enquired.

Ramirez hesitated. 'I will speak with you further on this matter at a later date, *menina*. For the present, things will continue as they are. And please—endeavour not to cause trouble between Miguel and his professor. Senhor Perez is not the most patient of men.'

Christina did not reply but walked towards the door. However, Ramirez was there before her, striding across the floor with his lithe, cat-like tread, swinging open the door and inclining his head as she passed through.

'Miguel will be on the patio in half an hour,' he advised her smoothly. '*Adeus, menina!*'

Christina felt indignation rising within her as she walked back along the corridor to the tiled hall. She was not used to being treated like an inconsequent child, and Ramirez's attitude infuriated her. She mounted the stairs to her room two at a time and once there slammed the door with childish impatience. What was she supposed to do here? Spend her days waiting to be summoned to the presence?

She stared at her reflection moodily, and then on impulse she unfastened the buttons of her blouse and stepped out of her skirt. She refused to remain unnoticed in her room. If Dom Carlos had nothing for her to do then it was up to her to find something, and now was as good a time as any to find out whether the lucid waters of the swimming pool were real or artificial like everything else here.

CHAPTER SIX

DONNA INEZ appeared on the patio while Christina was in the pool and she stared at the girl with obvious amazement. Christina smiled, refusing to allow the older woman's manner to daunt her, and Donna Inez had, perforce, to return the smile, albeit in rather a wintry fashion. She seated herself in the shade of the gallery on a basketwork lounger beside a glass-surfaced table, and presently a uniformed maid appeared with a tray of what appeared to be afternoon tea.

Deciding she had had enough for the present, Christina climbed out of the pool, dripping water all over its immaculately tiled rim. She wrung out her hair and then reaching for the towel which she had draped over a canvas chair she began to towel herself vigorously.

Donna Inez looked up from pouring her tea and encountered Christina's eyes upon her. For a moment she seemed to take in the appearance of Christina's slender young body in the white bikini she was wearing, and then she said in stiff tones:

'Will you join me for tea, Miss Ashley?'

Christina hesitated. She wanted to refuse, but could think of no valid reason for doing so, so donning the towelling jacket she had brought with her, she said: 'Thank you,' and walked round to where Donna Inez was seated.

'Milk or lemon?' queried Donna Inez politely, and Christina said: 'Milk, please,' before seating herself in another of the basketwork chairs.

After finishing pouring the tea Donna Inez lay back

in her chair studying the girl intently. 'Do you enjoy swimming, Miss Ashley?' she asked.

Christina refused one of the sugary biscuits Donna Inez proffered and then answered: 'Very much. I've never swum in a private pool before, though. It was quite a novelty.'

Donna Inez inclined her head. 'The pool is seldom used these days. Once my nephew used to give parties, bathing parties you understand, but nowadays ...' She shrugged her shoulders, and then as though regretting the confidence, she went on, more assuredly: 'I understand you attempted to thwart my nephew's instructions regarding Miguel's routine.'

Christina replaced her cup carefully in its saucer. 'I went to see Miguel while he was resting, yes,' she replied slowly.

Donna Inez clicked her tongue. 'Why did you do that, Miss Ashley? Surely I explained quite satisfactorily that Miguel would be free later in the afternoon?'

Christina bit her lip thoughtfully. 'I didn't see what harm I was doing. The boy was awake and restless. And besides, I'm not altogether convinced that so much resting is good for him.'

Donna Inez's lips twitched. 'You are not a doctor, Miss Ashley.'

Christina was tempted to reply that nor was she, but she restrained her natural indignation and lifted her cup again. 'It's—quite beautiful here, isn't it?' she said politely.

Donna Inez drew in her lips. Christina's abrupt change of topic had disconcerted her. 'Beautiful, *sim*,' she agreed, at last. 'Tell me something more Miss Ashley, what do you propose to do when your days at the university are over? What plans have you for the future?'

Christina relaxed. 'I'd like to teach,' she replied

simply.

'I see.' Donna Inez frowned. 'And what of marriage? Surely girls in England are as keen to fulfil their natural capabilities as Portuguese women are.'

'Some are, some aren't.' Christina half smiled. 'And some might say what are a woman's natural capabilities?' She shrugged. 'There is not such a conformist attitude towards marriage there as there is here. Women are permitted more freedom. They choose for themselves whether or not they desire a husband—a home—children!'

Donna Inez took another biscuit from the exquisitely thin bone china plate. 'Not all Portuguese women conform, Miss Ashley. We have our emancipated doctors—scientists—teachers! But in Portugal we place greater emphasis on femininity, I think. We are not so keen to dress as men do, to be treated as their equal in every way. We prefer our menfolk to remain chivalrous, gallant, you understand?'

Christina's smile widened. 'I hope I'm not giving you a poor impression of British womanhood,' she murmured mischievously.

Donna Inez looked a little put out at Christina's obvious refusal to take their conversation seriously, but she was saved from making any reply by the appearance of Senhor Perez, propelling Miguel in his wheelchair.

Miguel's face brightened considerably when he saw Christina and he insisted that Perez should place his chair next to hers. Perez cast a chilling glance in Christina's direction but obeyed his young charge's request, his eyes flickering appraisingly over the girl so that Christina felt like wrapping her towelling jacket closer about her.

'You have been swimming!' exclaimed Miguel, as Perez bowed politely to Donna Inez and departed.

Christina nodded. 'Yes. I've never swum in a private

pool before. It was quite exciting. Do you swim, Miguel?'

Donna Inez caught her breath at the question and Christina was aware that Miguel had heard that startled intake.

He shook his head now and leaning towards his aunt he said: 'May I have some tea, Tia Inez?'

Donna Inez looked gratified at the request and Christina sighed. How on earth was she supposed to make friends with Miguel if every time they were together someone else was present?

Getting to her feet, she said: 'I'll go and dress. Wait for me, Miguel.'

Miguel looked up with a smile now. 'Don't be long,' he advised her gently.

When she returned she was dressed in cream shorts and a navy crocheted sweater that had no sleeves and showed her firm breasts to advantage. Donna Inez looked scandalised, but Christina refused to be put off.

'Have you had tea, Miguel?' she asked, and at his startled nod, she went on: 'Then how would you like to show me the grounds? I haven't had the opportunity to look round at all.'

Miguel glanced doubtfully at his aunt, and Donna Inez clicked her tongue. 'It is too hot, *senhorita*. Perhaps tomorrow . . .'

Christina clenched her fists. 'We can walk in the shade of the trees,' she averred with determination. 'Can't we, Miguel?'

Miguel nodded, eager now to agree with her, but Donna Inez rose to her feet.

'I do not think Dom Carlos would approve of such an arrangement, *senhorita*,' she said stiffly.

Christina sighed. 'We are only going for a walk, *senhora*. What possible objections can anyone raise?' she took charge of Miguel's wheelchair. 'Are you comfortable, Miguel?'

'Miss Ashley!' Donna Inez's voice was cold. 'I do not like your attitude. I am not accustomed to being summarily ignored in this manner!'

Christina's fingers tightened on the handles of the chair. 'I'm sorry, *senhora*,' she responded politely, but it was obvious from the tone of her voice that she considered Donna Inez was behaving rather foolishly.

Donna Inez drew herself up to her full height and turning walked away into the *quinta*, her heels clicking sharply on the tiles of the patio. Miguel looked up. 'What do we do now—Christina?' he whispered.

'We go for a walk,' replied Christina, with a forced smile, 'Don't we?'

Miguel ran his tongue over his lips. '*Naturalmente*,' he replied, and a hint of a smile appeared in the dark eyes.

Christina relaxed suddenly. What did it matter what Donna Inez thought of her, or Ramirez himself for that matter, so long as Miguel began to enjoy life again instead of just enduring it?

The grounds immediately surrounding the *quinta* were extensive as Christina had known they would be. But what she had not been entirely prepared for was the wealth of beauty and colour that someone had painstakingly achieved in rose gardens and water gardens and terraces of sub-tropical foliage.

Beyond the surroundings of the *quinta* acres of parkland could be seen, thickly wooded in places where Miguel said it was still possible to come upon wild deer.

The gardens in front of the house swept down to the cliffs overlooking the sweep of private beach below where Christina had first encountered Dom Carlos Ramirez. She couldn't entirely dispel the quiver of awareness that ran through her as she recalled that encounter, and then Miguel distracted her attention, pointing out a small lift let into the cliff face which he said his uncle had had installed for his use.

'So we can go down to the beach!' exclaimed Christina, eagerly. 'Oh, that's marvellous, Miguel! I adore the sea, don't you?'

Miguel shrugged his thin shoulders. 'It's all right,' he conceded indifferently, and Christina sighed.

'Well, we will go down to the beach,' she asserted. 'Tomorrow perhaps.'

'If you'd like to do so.' Miguel was unmoved by her apparent enthusiasm, but Christina determined to change all that. She didn't quite know how she would do so, but somehow she had to succeed.

When they re-entered the patio they found it deserted and Christina wheeled Miguel's chair near to a lounger and collapsed into it lazily. 'Gosh!' she exclaimed. 'I could just strip off my clothes and plunge into that pool again. Don't you feel like that?'

Miguel bent his head. 'What would be the use?' he asked quietly, and Christina sat up, staring at him.

But just as she was about to speak, a maid appeared. She came across to them diffidently, and said: 'Dom Carlos wishes to speak with you, *senhorita*.'

Christina sighed with impatience. 'Right now?' she asked shortly.

'*Sim, senhorita.*'

'Oh, damn!' Christina rose to her feet looking down at Miguel. 'Will you wait here?'

Miguel nodded. 'All right.'

Christina smiled, and then looked at the maid. 'Where is Dom Carlos?'

'In his study, *senhorita*. You wish I should show you——'

'No—no, I know the way.'

Christina walked quickly across the patio and in through the french doors, across the lounge and into the hall. It was strange how quickly she had become familiar with the place and she found Dom Carlos's study without difficulty. After knocking, she heard his abrupt summons to enter, and opened the door.

Dom Carlos was seated at his desk as she entered, studying some papers he had taken from a file, but he rose to his feet at once and took in her appearance with narrowed eyes. All at once Christina was intensely conscious of the brief legs of her shorts, and the closeness of the sweater.

Then he indicated that she should sit in the armchair opposite. 'Please, sit down, *menina*.'

'I'd rather stand.' Christina hooked her thumbs into the belt at the back of her shorts.

Dom Carlos regarded her broodingly for several moments, and then he squared his shoulders and said: 'My aunt tells me you took Miguel on a tour of the grounds against her instructions.'

Christina saw no point in prevarication. 'That's right.'

Dom Carlos glanced down at the papers on his desk. 'I have told my aunt she must not interfere between you and Miguel,' he said, surprising a gasp from her parted lips. He looked up. 'You are shocked?'

Christina nodded. 'I thought you had brought me here to complain again,' she admitted.

Dom Carlos looked at her steadily. 'You would agree then that there was something to complain about?'

'Yes—no—that is—I just thought you might!' Christina felt ridiculously youthful.

He studied her flushed cheeks a moment longer and then went on: 'Nevertheless, I should be most grateful if you could behave a little less aggressively in my aunt's presence. She is not used to your—independent ways!'

Christina sighed. Somehow he always managed to put her in the wrong, whether directly or indirectly, and she realised she had little defence except insolence against a man like him. She could never hope to challenge him on his own terms.

'Is that all, *senhor*?' she asked now, her hands falling to her sides.

Dom Carlos frowned. 'Your hair is still damp, *menina*. Be careful you do not catch cold. The pool is not sea water.'

Christina stiffened her back and walked towards the door. Then on impulse she turned, surprising him behind her, in the process of coming to open the door for her with his innate courtesy. Stepping back, she said, rather jerkily:

'Would you have any objections if I had my meals with Miguel, *senhor*?'

Dom Carlos looked down at her, one hand raised to finger his scar almost absently. He raised his eyebrows and then shrugged his broad shoulders. 'Perhaps you might join him for lunch, *menina*. You will eat dinner with my aunt and myself. Occasionally Miguel joins us also.'

Christina sighed. 'Thank you.'

'That is not the answer you wanted, *menina*?'

Christina shook her head helplessly. 'Will you explain the position to Senhor Perez, *senhor*?'

'Of course.' Dom Carlos inclined his head. 'And perhaps tomorrow morning, while Miguel is occupied with his lessons, you might like to visit my library, *menina*. I have many books, some first editions, you understand, and perhaps they might be of some assistance to you in sustaining your university studies.'

'Thank you.' Christina's throat was dry and she moved to the door. Her employer swung it open for her for the second time that day and she passed through, but as he closed the door behind her she had the most absurd desire to burst into tears.

During the next few days Christina became accustomed to life at the *quinta*. She had imagined her days

106

would drag unbearably until Miguel appeared, but instead she found more than enough to interest her in the extensive library. The morning after her arrival, after breakfasting in her room, which seemed the usual practice at the *quinta*, a maid had been deputed to guide her to the library on the ground floor, and left alone Christina was soon absorbed in Portuguese history.

As arranged, she lunched with Miguel, and whether by accident or design, she could never be certain, Senhor Perez invariably took his meals in his room, leaving them alone together.

After lunch, she sunbathed until it was time for Miguel to join her and then they would sit and talk or roam the grounds, occasionally taking the lift down to the beach below.

But it was practically impossible to propel Miguel's chair on the beach, and consequently, short of asking Dom Carlos for help, she had, for the present, to be content to sit with Miguel and just look at the sea.

She thought she was making a little progress. Miguel would occasionally show interest in her talk of skin-diving or water-skiing, related from things Bruce had written to her, but following Dom Carlos's advice she did not press him too hard.

She swam regularly in the pool, much to Donna Inez's annoyance she was sure, but so long as Dom Carlos made no objections she did not care. The most arduous time of her day came in the evenings when she was expected to dine with Dom Carlos and his aunt. Donna Inez made no secret of her dislike for the younger girl, due no doubt to the fact that Dom Carlos seemed to be giving her free rein with Miguel, and the long meal was a period she hated. Only Dom Carlos ever addressed her direct, and Donna Inez made spiteful little innuendoes from time to time that Christina had the utmost difficulty in ignoring.

She invariably spent the meal covertly studying her employer, aware that for some inexplicable reason he intrigued her. Maybe it was that she had never met a man quite like him before, or perhaps it was simply a case of physical attraction, she wasn't sure. He did attract her, but then he was an attractive man, even with the disfiguring scar, and she knew she was curious to find out whether he ever relaxed completely. He never seemed to do so. He seemed constantly aloof, detached, remote from the people around him. Christina would have liked to have tried to penetrate that indifferent façade.

But that was not her purpose here, and besides, apart from these periods in the evenings she rarely saw her employer. He was a busy man, that much she gathered from Miguel's conversation, and from all accounts he had little time to spend in relaxation. Christina couldn't help but wonder whether there was a woman somewhere who saw infinitely more of him than his family did.

She had been given no regular time off since her arrival and while she realised that the greater part of the day was her own, she could hardly leave the *quinta* without Dom Carlos's permission.

One evening, about ten days after her arrival, she decided to tackle Dom Carlos about it at dinner. After all, apart from a brief telephone call to the hotel to tell her brother she was comfortably installed she had made no contact with him, and she wanted to go and see him. She thought she might go the following afternoon and take Miguel with her. No further mention had been made of Miguel giving up his lessons and they would have to go after his rest.

However, when she went down for dinner that evening she found Donna Inez alone at the table. Occasionally this had happened before, but tonight Christina had to say: 'Could you tell me where Dom Carlos is, *senhora?'*

Donna Inez looked at the girl coolly. 'He is dining with some friends of his, the Almedas, Miss Ashley. Why? Was there some especial reason why you wished to see him tonight?'

Christina shook her head and subsided into her chair. She didn't want to discuss her proposed plans with Miguel's aunt. She smiled politely and changed the subject. 'Hasn't it been a warm day, *senhora?* Rather thundery, don't you think?'

Donna Inez's nostrils flared delicately. 'You are finding the climate enervating, Miss Ashley?'

Christina bent her head to hide her smile. She had no doubt that Donna Inez hoped she was finding it too hot. It would give her a lever with which to persuade Dom Carlos to get rid of her.

'Not at all,' Christina replied now. 'I love the sun!'

Donna Inez wiped the corner of her mouth on a table napkin. 'A rather extravagant expression surely, *senhorita,*' she observed dryly. 'We Portuguese do not use love so freely as you do.'

Christina pressed her hands together in her lap. 'Very well then, I adore the climate,' she amended easily. 'And I'm enjoying my stay enormously.'

Donna Inez directed her attention to the shellfish on her plate. 'And do you think you are making any progress with Miguel?' she queried insinuatingly.

Christina sighed. 'That's difficult to say because I don't really know how interested he was in things before I arrived. But I think we get along well together and when I swim I sometimes think he would like to put on swimming trunks and join me.'

Donna Inez's lip curled a little. 'You swim a lot, Miss Ashley. I've noticed that your skin is becoming quite brown. Don't you mind?'

Christina glanced down at her golden tan. 'Why should I mind, *senhora?*'

Donna Inez raised her aristocratic eyebrows. 'Portuguese women guard their complexions, *senhorita*. A pale skin is to be admired.'

'But I am not Portuguese, *senhora*,' retorted Christina rather heatedly, annoyed that the older woman could constantly rub her up the wrong way.

'I had noticed,' observed Donna Inez, with a faint, mocking smile.

When the meal was over Christina escaped to the coolness of the gardens. Miguel had retired before dinner, which was often taken rather late at the *quinta*, and although he had occasionally joined them since her arrival, he had seemed ill at ease and silent in the company of both his uncle and his great-aunt.

Picking the petals from a magnolia with unaccustomed carelessness, Christina wondered what her friends at the university would think if they could see her now. She smiled, recalling the debates the students had held, sometimes extending far into the night, on the kind of revolutionary régimes they professed to admire. They would have deplored the system flourishing here in Porto Cedro, even though Christina had to admit to herself in all honesty that she had not found any discontentment here. With sudden insight she pondered the theory that revolution was a thing of the mind only, not to be pressed upon people simply because their ideas of happiness did not live up to those of others.

Deciding she was becoming too introspective, she went back to the *quinta*, and got ready for bed. But once between the silk sheets sleep would not come. She found herself wondering where and with whom her employer was dining. Was he with friends, or with some particular feminine company who found his cool detachment and cruel good looks as challenging as Christina did herself?

The following morning after breakfast, Christina made her way to Dom Carlos's study to ask him about her proposed trip to Porto Cedro. But when she got to the door of the room she found it open and the housekeeper Juana in the process of polishing the desk. She smiled politely at Christina as she stood hesitatingly in the doorway, and when Christina asked where Dom Carlos was, Juana explained that he was away for the day at the vineyards.

Christina sighed. How infuriating! All her plans seemed to be wasted. She glanced back as Juana resumed her task, and said, on impulse: 'Tell me, Juana, has Alfredo Seguin gone with Dom Carlos?'

Juana straightened, flexing her back muscles. '*Nao, senhorita*. Dom Carlos drives himself.'

'I see.' Christina's spirits lifted. 'Then where could I find Alfredo Seguin?'

Juana frowned. 'He will be at the garages, *senhorita*. He has an *apartamento* there.'

'Oh, thank you.' Christina smiled, and leaving the housekeeper, she found her way outside and round to where the garages were situated some few yards from the main building.

As luck would have it, Seguin was outside washing one of his employer's automobiles and he looked up in surprise when Christina approached. '*Bom dia*, Miss Ashley,' he said politely. 'Can I help you?'

Christina explained that she wanted to go and see her brother that afternoon and take Miguel with her. Alfredo Seguin frowned. 'Dom Carlos is away today, *senhorita*. Is he agreeable to this outing?'

Christina sighed. 'He has said I may take Miguel out,' she answered truthfully.

Seguin shrugged. 'Very well, *senhorita*. Would four o'clock be suitable?'

'Marvellous, thank you,' Christina smiled, and then walked back to the house.

She had decided to tell Donna Inez what she intended to do, but unfortunately Donna Inez was suffering from a headache and therefore Christina had to be content with sending a message with one of the servants as she could hardly invade the privacy of Donna Inez's rooms herself.

Miguel, when she told him at lunchtime, was interested. 'I've never been to an hotel before,' he said. 'What is it like? Is it very big?'

Christina smiled. 'No, it's rather small, actually. But I think you'll enjoy the outing. We might walk round the village. Would you like that?'

Miguel clasped his hands together. Already there were signs of a brightening in his thin features, and his appetite was improving, Christina had noted. At least when he ate with her he seemed to enjoy his food.

The outing began very successfully. Bruce was delighted to see her and he wheeled Miguel's chair into the hotel after Alfredo had lifted the boy into it. Sheila, too, conscious of Miguel's interested presence, was more friendly than usual, and she rushed about preparing afternoon tea for them, and generally behaving as though she was delighted to have guests.

Miguel blossomed under the concentrated interest shown in him and talked more than Christina had expected, smiling and laughing with her brother as though they had known one another for years.

Bruce would have made a wonderful father, thought Christina with a sigh, as she watched him describing the delights of underwater swimming to Miguel. He had the knack of reducing his terms to simple ones, and she could tell that Miguel was fascinated.

'Perhaps Miguel would like a trip on the boat one day,' Bruce suggested, glancing across at Christina questioningly.

Christina's eyes widened and she looked quickly at Miguel. 'Would you like that, Miguel?' she asked, hardly daring to hope that he might agree.

Miguel hesitated, pressing his lips together. 'But—but how could I?' he said at last. 'I mean——' He glanced down helplessly at the wheelchair.

Bruce made a dismissing gesture. 'I can carry you, Miguel,' he exclaimed smilingly. 'I promise not to drop you.' His eyes twinkled.

Miguel bit his lip, obviously fighting some inner battle within himself. 'Well——' he began slowly. 'If you think it would be—all right.'

Christina wanted to skip with excitement. 'Oh, we'll have a marvellous time, Miguel,' she cried. Then she turned to Bruce. 'When can you arrange it?'

Sheila came back into the room at that moment and looked questioningly at Christina's animated face. 'What's going on here?' she enquired lightly. 'What are you going to arrange, Bruce?'

Christina prayed Sheila would say nothing to spoil Miguel's anticipation, but she need not have worried. Sheila was too conscious of Miguel's illustrious relative to risk offending either of them, and she listened with interest to what Bruce had to say and then suggested that Christina ought to wait and fix a day with Miguel's uncle.

Christina had to be content with this, but she was eager to get Miguel interested in something other than intellectual pursuits. Once she could arouse a desire within him to be able to do the things other people could do she would be halfway towards success.

After tea was over, Christina said she would take Miguel for a walk round the village, and Bruce accompanied them. They gravitated towards the harbour, and Bruce showed the boy his boat. Miguel's interest had waned slightly at the knowledge that Christina would have to discuss the trip with Dom Carlos before it could be arranged, and Christina herself was anxious to sustain the relationship between her brother and the boy.

While they were by the harbour wall, Julio appeared and Christina turned to him in surprise, glad to see a familiar face.

'The new visitors have arrived, *senhor*,' Julio advised Bruce smilingly. 'The *senhora* sent me down to ask you to come back.'

Bruce sighed and looked regretfully at Miguel. 'I see.'

'Must you go?' asked Christina, unable to hide her disappointment. 'I wanted you to take Miguel aboard the boat.'

Bruce sighed. 'I'm afraid so. Another time——'

Julio frowned. 'If you will permit it, *senhor*, I could look after Christina and the boy.'

If Bruce thought anything of Julio's casual use of her Christian name, he did not show it, but he hesitated before replying. Looking at his sister, he said: 'It's after six, Chris. Don't you think it's about time you were heading back to the *quinta*?'

Christina shrugged. 'There's plenty of time,' she protested. Then she looked at Miguel. 'What do you want to do, Miguel?'

Miguel was infected by a little of her enthusiasm. 'I would like to stay a little longer,' he said.

Bruce glanced at his watch. 'Okay, okay, Julio, you're in charge. But just for fifteen minutes, Chris, do you hear? Then Julio will push Miguel's chair back to the hotel.'

Christina smiled in satisfaction. 'Thanks, Bruce.'

Bruce shook his head a trifle doubtfully, but then he turned and strode away towards the road leading up to the Hotel Inglês. Miguel watched him go and then looked at Christina. 'Well?' he said. 'Can we go on board?'

Christina's smile lifted the corners of her mouth. 'Why not? Julio!'

Julio was strong and lithe and it was no difficulty for him to lift Miguel's slight weight out of his chair and carry him across the gangway on to the motor launch. Miguel looked around him with interest, enjoying the rise and fall of the boat on the harbour swell.

The launch was a modern vessel, steered in much the same way as a car from a small pilot cabin above the sleeping quarters below. A wide windscreen gave a panoramic view to the driver and Christina longed to take Miguel out for a proper trip. But that would have to wait until Bruce could arrange it.

Julio carried Miguel into the lower compartment and set him down on the padded banquette that ran round the walls of the cabin. Christina followed them and Julio proceeded to show them the gear that was stowed away in the lockers for skin-diving. There were oxygen cylinders and face masks and snorkelling equipment, and Miguel was fascinated. Julio, in his way, was just as adept at putting the boy at his ease as Bruce had been, with the added advantage of being nearer Miguel's own age. Christina sat beside Miguel, watching his expressive face, eagerly planning ahead to the time when they would be able to persuade Miguel to put on swimming trunks and go into the water himself.

Julio had pulled on a face mask and was tugging flippers on to his feet to stride round the cabin like some sea monster causing Miguel and Christina to laugh uproariously when the launch rocked violently, as though someone had come aboard.

Julio looked questioningly at Christina and she was shaking her head when the sliding door to the cabin was thrust open, and Dom Carlos Martinho Duarte de Ramirez stood in the aperture, glaring at them with unconcealed anger.

CHAPTER SEVEN

IMMEDIATELY Julio pulled off the face mask and fumbled to unfasten the flippers, feeling rather ridiculous, while Christina chewed nervously at her lip, watching Miguel rather apprehensively.

Dom Carlos gripped the door jamb with long taut fingers and continued to regard them all icily. 'What is going on here, Miss Ashley?' he demanded fiercely, more angry than she had ever seen him, his eyes raking her shirt and shorts contemptuously. 'Am I expected to condone this situation?'

'Tio Carlos, don't be angry!' Miguel spoke before Christina could think of any suitable reply. 'Christina —and Julio—were just showing me the equipment for underwater exploration. There is no cause for alarm.'

Dom Carlos's eyes narrowed at Miguel's unconscious use of Christina's name. 'Be silent, Miguel!' he snapped shortly. 'I addressed my question to Miss Ashley, not to you!'

Miguel's thin face flushed scarlet, and Christina felt an angry resentment that Ramirez had the power to reduce Miguel to an embarrassed schoolboy. But what else could she have expected from a man who could do much the same to her?

'Surely you can see for yourself, Dom Carlos, that this is a perfectly innocent expedition,' she said sharply. 'My brother was with us until a few minutes ago when he was summoned back to the hotel. We were going back there ourselves almost immediately. There is absolutely no cause for alarm——'

Dom Carlos looked at her coldly. 'You think not? Not even when I see my nephew's wheelchair standing empty beside the harbour wall?'

Christina put a hand to her mouth. 'Oh!' she said faintly.

Dom Carlos turned his attention to Julio who had succeeded in shedding the diving gear and was presently occupied in putting it hastily away again. 'You can go back to the hotel, Julio, and tell Seguin to return to the *quinta*. I will escort my nephew home.'

Julio straightened, almost banging his head in the process. '*Sim, senhor*,' he responded politely, awkwardly making a kind of salute. '*Immediatemente, senhor!*'

Dom Carlos stood aside to allow him to leave and with a helpless shrug at the others Julio had to comply. They heard his footsteps as he crossed the deck and then the receding sound as he traversed the gangplank to the quay. Only then did Dom Carlos enter the cabin and look down at his nephew rather thoughtfully.

'*Pois bem*, Miguel, you have enjoyed yourself today?'

Miguel's doubtful expression disappeared. 'Very much, Tio Carlos,' he exclaimed eagerly. 'I like the boat—I like the way it moves—and Julio made me laugh,' he finished defensively.

Dom Carlos flicked a speck of dust from his immaculate grey jacket, and glanced at Christina, his eyes enigmatic. 'And you, Miss Ashley? Did you not consider I deserved prior warning of this—outing?'

Christina sighed. 'I tried to tell you, but you weren't around. Besides, you did say you would put Seguin at our service if we required him.'

She looked down at her sandal-clad feet, annoyed at having to make these childish explanations. 'I expected we would be back before you. I'm sorry if you saw the chair and jumped to the wrong conclusions.'

'Are you, Miss Ashley? Are you, really?' He looked cynical. '*Portanto*, Miguel, you would perhaps like me to take you sailing one day?'

Miguel looked quickly at Christina. 'Christina's brother—that is—Senhor Ashley—he is to take me out in his boat—this boat,' he replied unhappily.

'I see.' Dom Carlos straightened his shoulders. 'You have arranged this, Miss Ashley?'

Christina sighed again. 'I've arranged nothing, *senhor*. Naturally I should have consulted you before doing anything.'

'And if I should not have been—around? What then, *menina*?'

'I should have left a message days before,' retorted Christina.

Dom Carlos considered her for a moment longer and then bent to Miguel. 'Come, *meu filho*, I will carry you to the quay.'

Christina allowed them to leave the cabin first and then followed them, closing the door behind her. She felt disappointed and depressed and she wondered what Bruce would think when they did not return to the hotel. He would know the reasons why, of course, Julio would explain them, but right now Christina would have been glad of Bruce's support.

Dom Carlos deposited Miguel in his chair and then took charge of it himself, waiting until Christina came to join them. She felt incongruous beside his elegantly clad figure in her casual shirt and shorts, but she forced an indifferent expression to her face.

Dom Carlos's car was parked at the foot of the road leading up to the hotel. It was a car Christina had not seen before, a sleek cream convertible, with wide comfortable black seats. Dom Carlos put Miguel and his folding chair into the back and then swung open the front passenger side door for Christina. She had, perforce, to climb in, but she was intensely conscious of his thigh only inches away from hers all the way back to the *quinta*.

After Miguel had been left in the charge of his personal servant, Dom Carlos turned to Christina who had been about to disappear up to her room until dinner time.

'Come,' he said briefly. 'I wish to speak with you.'

Christina hunched her shoulders. 'I wanted to shower and change before dinner, *senhor*,' she protested.

'What I have to say will not take long, *menina*,' he returned smoothly, and indicated that she should lead the way to his study.

Christina accepted his adjunct to sit down when she reached the study. In truth she was feeling inordinately tired, and in no state for a verbal confrontation with Dom Carlos.

However, Dom Carlos came straight to the point. 'I did not wish to embarrass you, *menina*, while Miguel was there, but I do not wish you to spend any more time alone in the company of Julio Durante.'

Christina gasped. 'I beg your pardon, but what did you say?'

'I think you heard what I said very well, *menina*. I do not wish you to spend time alone with Julio.'

Christina stared at him impatiently. 'But why? I—I like him. So does Miguel. And I think he likes me.'

'Most assuredly he does, *menina*. You are a—*novidade*. A novelty! But it is not fitting that you should spend your time with him.'

Christina frowned. 'You're talking about this afternoon, of course.'

'Of course.'

Christina wrinkled her nose. 'Miguel was with us this afternoon,' she declared.

'Miquel can in no way be termed a *companheiro*, *menina*, a chaperon!'

'I don't need a chaperon, *senhor*!'

'I disagree.'

His tone was inflexible and as he reached for a cigar she wondered why she bothered to argue with him. As always he would have the final word. Wanting to shock him out of that cool detachment, she burst out, rather childishly: 'Julio and I have been swimming together—alone!'

Dom Carlos looked up from lighting his cigar. 'I know,' he said infuriatingly.

Christina was taken aback. 'You *know*?'

Dom Carlos half smiled. 'Of course. There is very little going on in Porto Cedro that I am not aware of, *menina*.'

Christina got abruptly to her feet. 'Is that all, then?' she asked rudely.

'No. Not quite.' Dom Carlos drew deeply on his cigar. 'As Miguel shows an interest in sailing. I will make arrangements for a trip possibly next week in my yacht, *Turbilhao*.'

Christina looked doubtful. 'Do I take it you will be taking Miguel yourself, *senhor*?'

Dom Carlos inclined his head. 'Of a certainty, *menina*. I will let you know nearer the time what day we will choose.'

Christina moved a little way towards the door. Then she turned and looked back at him. 'Do you think I might spend the day with my brother then, *senhor*?' she asked tentatively.

Dom Carlos moved round the desk to join her. 'You will accompany Miguel and myself, naturally,' he said, and now there was a trace of impatience in his strange tawny eyes. 'What is wrong, *menina*? Does the prospect of a day spent in my company appal you?'

'Of course not. I just thought——' Christina halted, sighing. 'And what of a chaperon, *senhor*?'

Dom Carlos's jaw stiffened. 'None will be called for,

120

menina. I am your employer, the uncle of your charge, a man, moreover, old enough to be your father.' He turned away, thrusting a hand into the pocket of his trousers. 'I am long past the need for dalliance with members of the opposite sex, so you need have no fears on that score.'

Christina pressed her lips together. Again she was conscious of his need to constantly sustain his own awareness of his disfigurement and she wished passionately that there was some way she could prove to him that he was no less of a man because of it.

But she dared not suggest such a thing in so many words. Whatever his inner feelings might be to him she was simply a contemporary of his nephew's, capable only of the most shallow emotions. And probably her attitude and the way she dressed served to remind him forcibly of her youthfulness.

Now he moved to open the door for her as usual, but as she moved past him, he said: 'I have observed that Miguel addresses you by your Christian name.'

Christina halted, looking up at him in surprise. She had not been this close to him before, and she had an almost overwhelming urge to touch the harsh scar on his cheek and smooth the lines of cynicism from his eyes. His hair lay thick and smooth against his head, and the long black lashes concealed the expression in his eyes.

She sensed that he stiffened under that intent appraisal and realised with a feeling of incredulity that for a brief moment she was in command of the situation. She wondered what he would do if she put out a hand and touched him, and her lips parted involuntarily. His eyes which had been fixed on some point above her head suddenly moved to her face, and for several seconds she held his gaze.

It was a tantalising experience, doubly so, for until that moment she had imagined Dom Carlos to be completely immune from normal physical awareness. But with insight she realised that beneath his mask of indifference he was merely holding himself in iron control. A thrill of excitement ran along her veins, and then dissolved as he moved away from her, saying almost chillingly:

'I have no objections, *menina*. As you obviously give this privilege cheaply.'

Christina closed her nails on her palms, but refrained from making any retort. Instead, she walked out of the study, uncaring what construction he might place on her actions.

It was almost two weeks before Dom Carlos was able to arrange the trip on his yacht. A crisis at the vineyards took him away most days, and sometimes Christina did not see him for several days at a time.

But Miguel seemed not to mind. With Seguin's assistance she had succeeded in taking him on to the private beach below the *quinta* and she knew he enjoyed watching her strip off her clothes and dive into the creaming waters of the Atlantic.

Later she would stretch out on the sands beside him, sunbathing, and Miguel had been persuaded to shed his concealing rugs and expose his painfully thin legs to the healing warmth of the sun.

Occasionally, they would tease one another and play games and it was during these periods of rough and tumble that she sensed Miguel was using muscles he had not attempted to use for years. She hoped that one day he would be sufficiently excited to become aware of these sensations for himself, but for the moment it was enough to infuse enthusiasm into his voice.

Christina enjoyed the weekends most, for then she was allowed all of Miguel's time, and during the long lazy days they learned a lot about one another. Miguel didn't speak of the plane crash yet that had killed his parents, but he did speak of the time before he was paralysed and Christina knew this was encouraging.

Twice they visited Bruce in Porto Cedro. Miguel always enjoyed these outings, but Christina had had to tell him that his uncle was planning a trip for them on his yacht and therefore the proposed trip with Bruce was temporarily postponed. Miguel had been patently disappointed and Christina wondered why. She would have thought Dom Carlos's yacht was far preferable to Bruce's motor launch, but one could never presuppose anything with Miguel.

Two days before the planned yacht trip, Donna Inez went out for the day to see some relatives, and as Dom Carlos was away also, Christina and Miguel had the *quinta* almost to themselves. Seguin was there, of course, always willing to help with Miguel, and on Christina's instructions he had put the boy on one of the air beds beside the pool to watch Christina in the water.

Miguel was beginning to look less strained, less pale, his limbs responding to the continued warmth of the sun. Although she had never discussed it with anyone, Christina could tell he was slowly coming to life again, and while the knowledge excited her it also brought it home to her quite disturbingly that Miguel was going to miss her terribly when these three months were over. Already she had been at the *quinta* nearly a month and the time was passing terribly quickly. What would he do when she had to leave? Who would there be to befriend him then? Donna Inez? Dom Carlos? He seemed to respond more quickly out of their company, and this was a shattering thought.

Christina swam to the rim of the pool and Miguel stretched out a hand and caught one of hers. Christina looked up at him mischievously. 'Aren't you afraid I'll pull you in?' she teased.

Miguel's eyes became shadowed. Then he squeezed

her fingers tightly. 'I—I have some swimming trunks,' he said hesitantly. 'Do you suppose—do you suppose a rubber float would support me—in—in the water?'

Christina hid her excitement, saying almost casually. 'I don't see why not. Do you want to come in?'

Miguel nodded. Then he sighed and lay back on the air bed, some of his enthusiasm draining away. 'It's no use though, is it? I couldn't swim with you.'

Christina bit her lip. 'There's more to being in the water than swimming!' she exclaimed.

Miguel propped himself up on his elbow. 'I'd make a fool of myself.'

Christina sighed. 'I do that all the time.'

Miguel smiled. 'No, you don't. You're always—oh, I don't know—marvellous! *Happy!*'

'I thought you were happy too.' Christina scrambled out of the water, dripping some on his bare legs. In shorts and a casual knitted shirt he looked exactly like any other boy. Even his legs, now that the sun could get at them, were losing their pallor.

Miguel looked up at her tanned healthy body, smooth and rounded in the navy blue bikini. He shaded his eyes. 'I want to swim with you,' he said helplessly.

'Then shall I tell Seguin?'

Miguel sighed and looked around. 'Tia Inez won't come back, will she?'

'No. She's away for the day. And Senhor Perez went in to Faro after lunch. Why? Don't you want them to see you?'

'No.' Miguel bent his head. 'Tia Inez pities me. I don't need their pity.'

Christina made no comment on this. 'I'll tell Seguin then,' she said, and Miguel nodded slowly.

Christina ran across the patio and into the *quinta*, uncaring that she dropped water on to the exquisitely polished floors. She found the telephone in the hall and rang Seguin's apartment at the garages.

He came at once, as eager as she was to do anything to aid Miguel's recovery.

Christina smiled at him as he lifted Miguel into his wheelchair to take him up to his room to change. 'Do you have swimming trunks, Alfredo?' she asked.

Seguin looked taken aback. 'But of course, *senhorita.*'

'Then perhaps you could join us?' Christina suggested, and Miguel nodded, too.

Seguin hesitated and then shrugged. 'Dom Carlos will not——'

Christina interrupted him impatiently. 'Dom Carlos is not here. I am. And besides, I shall need your help.'

Seguin gave a faint smile. 'Very well, *senhorita,*' he bowed his head in mock humility. 'Just give us a few minutes.'

At Alfredo's suggestion, Miguel made his first venture into the water holding securely to the air bed he had been lounging on earlier. It took him several minutes to gain enough confidence to master this art of supporting himself alone, but gradually the lift of the water enabled him to do so and a look of excited achievement and anticipation brought the colour to his face.

Christina was glad of Alfredo's encouragement. Somehow Miguel had accepted the man's presence and his unobtrusive offers of assistance. Christina knew she could never have managed without him.

It was an exhilarating experience watching Miguel. They were under no illusions that he had found the use of his legs again, but he was using muscles almost involuntarily that he had not used for years. They had achieved a major breakthrough and the glances they shared were tinged with a natural feeling of pride.

Not wanting to overtire Miguel, Christina insisted he came out of the water at the end of half an hour, and the boy protested roundly.

'But I'm just beginning to enjoy it!' he exclaimed disappointedly.

'All the more reason to come out now before you begin to wear yourself out,' asserted Christina firmly. 'There's always tomorrow, you know.'

'Tia Inez will be here tomorrow,' said Miguel gloomily. 'And Senhor Perez—and my uncle!'

Alfredo made an expressive gesture at Christina and she shook her head helplessly. However, Miguel permitted himself to be lifted out on to the side of the pool and sat for a few moments dangling his feet in the water while Alfredo towelled himself dry and put on his shirt and trousers over his swimming trunks.

Christina, stretched out on the pool's mosaic-tiled rim, looked up at the man gratefully. 'Thanks,' she said, with a smile. 'I couldn't have managed without you.'

Alfredo smiled in return. 'It was a pleasure, *senhorita*.'

Christina sat up, wrapping her arms round her drawn-up knees. 'Do you suppose we could do this again—in the sea?' She looked quickly at Miguel who was pulling a towelling robe about his shoulders. 'No one would see you there, Miguel.'

Miguel frowned. 'Could we?' He looked up at Alfredo. 'Could we?'

Alfredo sighed, and then shrugged. 'I somehow have the feeling that your uncle will object, Miguel.'

Miguel hunched his shoulders. 'We don't have to tell him.'

'No, we don't,' agreed Christina, getting to her feet. 'Oh, Alfredo, it's exciting, don't you think?'

Alfredo gave her a smile. 'If you say so,' he answered teasingly, but she knew he felt the same.

Putting Miguel into his wheelchair, he wheeled him away to change, and Christina took a deep breath before diving headlong into the pool again.

That evening at dinner she asked Dom Carlos whether Seguin could take herself and Miguel driving the following afternoon. Dom Carlos raised no objections, but Christina had the feeling that he wasn't altogether listening to what she was saying. Of late he had seemed to withdraw into himself at mealtimes and not even his aunt was capable of arousing more than a monosyllabic reply from him.

In consequence, the following afternoon, Seguin drove to a quiet cove some distance along the coast and they repeated their success of the pool. Miguel seemed eager to show what he could do, and Christina wondered whether she ought not to confide what they were doing to Dom Carlos. After all, their methods were very primitive. No doubt given the right surroundings and the right equipment, real therapy could be practised on Miguel's wasted young limbs, and yet wasn't that exactly what had been tried before without success?

It was a problem, and one she couldn't solve alone.

The following morning Christina awoke with a strange feeling of foreboding and for a moment she couldn't understand why she should feel this way. Then she remembered. Today was the day Dom Carlos was taking them out on his yacht, and she felt convinced it would be a trial to all of them.

She hesitated over what to wear. In the normal way she would have worn shorts as usual, but for once she thrust them aside and put on a navy pleated skirt and an apricot blouse, plaiting her hair into one thick braid. Underneath she was wearing the white bikini and she stuffed a towel into the canvas bag she carried.

After breakfasting in her room as usual she made her way downstairs and encountered Dom Carlos in the hall. She stopped short at the sight of him. In cream shorts and a cream cotton shirt that fastened with laces at his throat he looked vastly different from the immaculately clad *fidalgo* she was used to seeing. She could see, too, that his legs and arms were tanned a deep brown and she realised despite her impressions of him that he did spend quite a lot of time out in the open air.

Ignoring her speculative gaze, he said: *'Bom dia, menina.* You are ready?'

Christina nodded. 'Yes, *senhor.*'

'Good.' Dom Carlos nodded towards the front of the building. 'Miguel and Seguin are waiting on the terrace.'

'Seguin!' Christina couldn't prevent the involuntary ejaculation.

'Sim, Seguin. He acts as crew for me.'

'Oh, I see.' Christina swallowed hard. For a moment she had thought he knew of their efforts on Miguel's behalf.

'So, shall we go?'

'Yes. Of course.'

Christina walked quickly across the hall and out on to the terrace. It was already very warm and she saw that Miguel was wearing only a light shirt and shorts. Seguin smiled at her and Christina tried to relax. But she was apprehensive and she couldn't help it.

They drove to the harbour at Porto Cedro in Dom Carlos's car. He explained on the way that the yacht was usually moored in the boatyard not far from the *quinta,* but it would be easier to take Miguel aboard from the quay.

Although by now Christina had become accustomed to living in the medieval luxury of the *quinta,* and had accepted the evidence of Dom Carlos's absolute wealth and authority, she was still unprepared for the sleek opulence of his yacht. *Turbilhao* rocked gently on her moorings, a forty-foot ketch gleaming in the morning sunlight.

Miguel's wheelchair was stowed below in the comfortable cabin and Miguel himself was made comfortable aft on the cushioned banquette. Like Bruce's launch the yacht had a powerful motor, and Dom Carlos used this to manoeuvre the vessel out of the harbour. Several fishermen waved to them and shouted a greeting, and Dom Carlos responded to all of them with his innate politeness.

Christina stood beside Miguel, unable to sit down. A surge of pure excitement was rising inside her, and she could not suppress it. It was a glorious morning after all, and heading out into the deep waters of the Atlantic, the wind lifting her hair, the sun warm upon her back, was wholly exhilarating.

Seguin, dressed in cotton trousers and a thin shirt, had stood in the bow to release the mooring, and now he walked along the side of the yacht, dropping down on to the deck to approach them smilingly.

'*Pois bem*, Miguel,' he said. 'You are not sorry you came?'

Miguel lifted his eyes to the chauffeur. 'Sorry? No,' he shook his head, but Christina was aware that there was not the enthusiasm in his voice that there should have been.

'It's marvellous!' she exclaimed. 'Where are we going?'

'Where do you want to go?'

The unexpected sound of Dom Carlos's voice behind her startled Christina so that she swung round, almost overbalancing in the process. Dom Carlos put out a hand and steadied her and for a brief moment his hard fingers were against her flesh and she quivered violently. Then she was free and he was bending down to his nephew with intense concern.

'Well, Miguel,' he challenged. 'Where would you like to go?'

Miguel's thin face flushed. 'I—I have no idea, Tio

129

Carlos. Anywhere you like, of course.' The formality in his voice was evident and Dom Carlos straightened, his jaw tightening.

Christina, watching this interchange, wished that Miguel were more like a normal boy. Couldn't he see that his uncle was trying to treat him as an equal?

Taking the initiative, she said: 'Could we go somewhere where we might swim later?'

Dom Carlos turned his attention to her then, his tawny eyes disturbingly intense. He had the knack of devoting his whole attention to a person so that Christina wanted to back away from that concentrated scrutiny.

'There is a cove further along the coast,' he said. 'It is only accessible by sea. The cliffs are very high and unscalable, you understand. But the sand shelves steeply, and it is ideal for all kinds of water sport.' He glanced up at the blue arc above them momentarily. 'We could water-ski——' his gaze dropped to her again, '—or skin-dive. That was what you were interested in, was it not?'

Christina's eyes widened. 'You skin-dive, *senhor*?'

Dom Carlos smiled, his teeth very white against the dark tan of his face. 'I do. Does that surprise you? Did you think I spent all my waking moments working?'

Christina spread a casual hand. 'I—I never thought about it, *senhor*.'

'Did you not?' His tone was sceptical, and she sensed that he knew exactly what she had thought about him.

To her relief he summoned Alfredo and they went forward to cut the engine and break out the sails. In the keen breeze the yacht responded powerfully, its bow breaking through the blue water at an increasing pace, creating a wake of white foam behind them. Christina had never experienced the thrill of sailing before, of being at the mercy of the elements, and she looked down at Miguel excitedly.

Even Miguel seemed more at his ease. The look of remote formality was leaving him and he gripped the side of the vessel staring down into the clear waters below.

Dom Carlos was only using one of *Turbilhao*'s sails, limiting her speed. Controlling a vessel of its size at full sail would be an all-absorbing occupation, and Christina realised her employer would not risk such a practice with Miguel aboard.

The sun was tempered now by the breeze off the water, but it was still hot and Christina took off her blouse revealing the top of her bikini. She curled up on the banquette beside Miguel and leaning over trailed her hand in the water, smiling at the boy.

'Well?' she said softly. 'Are you enjoying it?'

Miguel shrugged. 'Who would not?'

'That's not the answer I wanted to hear, Miguel, and you know it.' Christina drew up her knees, resting her chin on them. 'Why do you not relax and enjoy yourself? Are you going to swim today?'

'*Swim!*' Miguel was scathing. 'I don't—*swim!*'

Christina sighed. 'You know what I mean.' She shook her head. 'Miguel, can't you see that all your body needs is a chance to be used—to be practised upon? Every time you enter the water—every time you do something with muscles that haven't been used for years you create a precedent, and sooner or later those muscles will begin to respond normally again.'

'No!' Miguel was abrupt.

'Why?'

'Because I don't want to walk again.'

Christina glanced surreptitiously round to make sure their conversation was not being overheard, but Dom Carlos and Alfredo were talking together, smoking the cigars that Dom Carlos favoured.

'What do you mean—you don't want to walk again?' she cried impatiently.

Miguel pressed his lips together. 'You wouldn't understand.'

'Try me!'

Miguel shook his head and sighed. 'It is a lovely day,' he murmured.

'Oh, *Miguel*!' Christina hugged her knees in exasperation. 'You've enjoyed going into the water these past couple of days, I know you have!'

Miguel bent his head. 'I know.'

'Well then?'

He looked up at her, his dark eyes troubled. 'Did you know that before the accident my uncle was betrothed to a woman called Sara Almeda?'

Christina drew her brows together. 'No. How could I? Your uncle doesn't confide in me.'

Miguel ran his finger along the rim of the vessel. 'I thought perhaps—Tia Inez——' He sighed. 'After the accident, she broke their betrothal.'

Christina felt a twinge of impatience. 'Did she? Why are you telling me all this?'

Miguel sighed again. 'I don't know. Don't you think it's rather sad?'

Christina made a moue with her lips. 'I don't know. It rather depends. If she broke their engagement she must have had a reason for doing so.'

Miguel dug his nail into the steel rim. 'She did. She couldn't bear his disfigurement.'

Christina raised her eyebrows. 'Indeed? Then it's probably for the best that she broke the engagement.'

'Why?'

'She sounds a rather shallow sort of person.'

'Do you think so?' Miguel looked at her intently.

'Of course. Besides, surely your uncle could have had plastic surgery.'

Miguel bent his head again. 'He could. But he wouldn't.'

Christina could imagine that. Dom Carlos Martinho

Duarte de Ramirez would never beg for anything, and for him the fact that this woman could not accept him as he was would be sufficient to arouse his arrogance.

'What has all this to do with you anyway?' she asked now.

Miguel lifted his shoulders and then let them fall pitifully. 'I don't know.'

Christina uttered an exclamation. 'Yes, you do!' she contradicted him impatiently. 'You haven't just been telling me about your uncle's unhappy love affair for no reason!'

'I just wanted you to know.' Miguel put out a hand and stroked her bare shoulder. 'I'm sorry if I've made you angry, Christina.'

'You haven't made me angry!' retorted Christina, and even as she did so she became aware of Dom Carlos approaching them along the deck.

His gaze flickered over Christina's brief apparel, and then alighted on his nephew. 'Look, Miguel,' he said, speaking in English for Christina's benefit. 'Look, over there! That's where we are making for.'

Christina and Miguel both looked. Ahead of them a rocky promontory jutted out some distance into the ocean forming a natural basin within its jagged formation. Further in shore the water paled to a translucent blue-green, the white sand of the beach still visible beneath the shallows. Edging the beach, the cliffs were tall, impregnable bastions of grey-gold rock, interspersed here and there with mossy growth and stunted grasses. The ocean surged constantly along the line of rocks and there was a soft hissing sound as the foam sucked greedily at their base. It was a suntrap, completely unspoiled and completely deserted.

Christina saw Miguel's look of undisguised anticipation and relaxed. Even Miguel could not maintain indifference against such an onslaught of pure untrammelled beauty, and she turned to his uncle, wanting him to share this moment.

But Dom Carlos was already looking at Miguel, his lean dark face twisted, his eyes tormented, and Christina wondered with a sinking sense of despair what it was that drove these two apart at a time when they should have been closest.

CHAPTER EIGHT

They had lunch in the luxurious cabin of the yacht, anchored off the deserted cove. Alfredo had proved himself an adept chef, and they enjoyed fresh melon, omelettes and salad, and fruit and icecream before reaching the coffee stage. Alfredo ate with them, and it was all very relaxed and enjoyable, the only sounds being the lap-lap of the water against the side of the vessel and the screeching cry of the seabirds overhead.

Dom Carlos and Alfredo were discussing the techniques of underwater exploration, and Dom Carlos told them of the occasion when he had joined an expeditionary party in the West Indies on the trail of a sunken Spanish galleon. They had spent weeks examining a wreck, but had only come up with a handful of gold coins. Someone else had been there before them and the treasures of gold and silver plate were lost for ever.

Christina was fascinated. This was an entirely different facet of Dom Carlos's character to her, and she suspected to Miguel also. Before his sister's death and his subsequent guardianship of Miguel he had led quite an adventurous life. He had been to Africa and South America, and knew a considerable amount about antiquities. Christina thought it was a pity he didn't talk like this in Miguel's presence more often. Didn't he realise that the boy found the description of his trips wholly absorbing, and that Miguel was like any other boy in this respect? With insight, she began to wonder whether Miguel might not respond more actively to therapy were he to have the prospect of such activities in view himself. But instead, Dom Carlos treated him like an invalid, encouraged him to talk about the things he could do, instead of those he *might* be able to do in the future.

When lunch was over Dom Carlos insisted that Miguel rest in the cabin for a while. Christina saw no objections in this. Miguel had had a strenuous morning compared to his usual routine, and he was not sorry to stretch out on one of the comfortable bunks.

Christina herself insisted on doing the washing up in the tiny galley while Alfredo and Dom Carlos went on deck to relax in the sun.

When she passed through the cabin again on her way to the deck, she found Miguel was already asleep, and she smiled at the relaxed curve of his mouth. Whatever happened, she was certain she was right to treat Miguel with less fragility.

On deck, Alfredo had rigged up a canvas awning, and he and his employer were engrossed in checking a pair of oxygen cylinders in the shade. Dom Carlos glanced at her as she walked uncertainly towards them, and then said: 'If you rest for a while, *menina*, you can swim later.'

'Thank you.' Christina's tone was sardonic. Did he think she was an imbecile, incapable of realising that she shouldn't swim immediately after the meal?

She stretched out on the engine housing in the full glare of the sun, sliding sunglasses on to her nose. The heat never troubled her, and she wriggled out of her skirt and exposed her legs and midriff to the glare.

A few moments later a shadow fell across her, and she opened her eyes to find Dom Carlos standing looking down at her.

'It is too hot to stay here,' he said censoriously, his eyes flickering over her slender body. 'Come into the shade of the awning. There is plenty of room and it is much more pleasant.'

Christina sighed, propping herself up on one elbow. 'Strange as it may seem to you, the sun does not bother me,' she said. 'Besides, I rubbed some lotion into my skin before we left this morning.'

'Nevertheless, you do not normally stay out in the heat of the day,' he said insistently. 'I have watched you in the pool and out of it and you usually wait until the sun is past its zenith.'

Christina felt disturbed at his words. She had not been aware of him noticing what she did.

'So?' she managed tautly.

'So do as I say,' he said quietly. 'I should not care to see you suffer the agonies of burnt flesh.'

Christina made a helpless movement of her shoulders, and got to her feet, swaying a little as the yacht rocked with her movements. He steadied her, as before, his hands gripping her forearms for a moment, and she looked up at him compulsively. She was aware of him with every fibre of her being and she wondered wildly what he would do if she pretended to over-balance and fell against him. It was a terrible temptation imagining herself caught in his arms, close against the hard strength of his lean body.

But Dom Carlos's jaw had tightened, and without a word he released her and strode back to where Alfredo Seguin was sitting.

Christina was forced to join them, but for a while they ignored her, talking together in their own language, discussing the possibilities of diving in these waters. Christina caught the gist of their conversation and then lay back idly, growing sleepy in the salt air and sunshine. But she could not forget that Dom Carlos was only a few inches away from her, and thoughts of him plagued her mind.

She recalled what Miguel had told her that morning. She wondered what manner of woman Sara

Almeda must be to break her engagement to Dom Carlos because of his injuries. And then Christina remembered that she had heard that name—Almeda—before. The night she had wanted to see Dom Carlos, to ask him about taking Miguel to see Bruce, Donna Inez had said that he was dining with the Almedas. She wondered whether this was the same family. It was possible if Sara Almeda had not married that she still lived with her parents. Girls of Dom Carlos's class did not branch out alone and get their own apartments as girls of good family did in England. On the contrary, it was very likely that Sara did still share the family home.

Christina rolled on to her stomach, glancing across at Dom Carlos. He was stretched out lazily beside Alfredo, a cigar between his teeth, tightening the valve on one of the cylinders. He didn't look like a man made bitter because the only woman he had ever loved had left him, and yet Christina knew that it was possible he could hide that as he hid his other emotions.

She cupped her chin on her knuckles, pondering how anyone could be cruel enough to tell a man that he no longer lived up to their physical expectations of him. It was ridiculous to suggest that Dom Carlos was any less of a man with his scar. To Christina, never having known him without it, it was an integral part of his personality.

She was shaken out of her reverie some time later by unaccustomed movement of the boat, and she opened her eyes to see Alfredo strapping oxygen cylinders to his back. He had flippers on his feet and goggles were pushed up his forehead.

Christina blinked and took off her sunglasses, sitting up with interest. Dom Carlos, who had been helping the other man to get ready, turned and glanced at her.

'You wish to swim now, *menina*?' he asked.

Christina frowned. 'What are you going to do, Alfredo?'

Alfredo smiled, examining the mouthpiece. 'I am going to play tennis, what else?' he challenged mockingly.

Christina scrambled to her feet. 'Could I—could I do that?'

Dom Carlos looked her up and down. 'Not immediately, no,' he shook his head.

Christina sighed. 'Why?'

'One must learn slowly. In the shallows. One must learn to breathe properly. Can you swim underwater?'

Christina frowned. 'A little.'

Dom Carlos tipped his head on one side. 'Then use the snorkelling equipment. That is best for beginners.'

Christina wrinkled her nose and looked over the side. The water around the vessel was a deep green, and very inviting. She had never swum from a boat before, and the knowledge that the depth of water below them was far greater than any she had ever swum in was all the more exciting.

Alfredo balanced on the side of the yacht and then somersaulted backwards into the water. He disappeared beneath the spreading ripples of his own entrance and Christina stared down longingly. What wonders waited in those translucent depths that she would possibly never see?

She looked at Dom Carlos. He was still dressed in his shirt and shorts although he had unfastened the laces at the neck to reveal the broad chest beneath and the beginning of the matt of hairs which darkened it. He seemed to be tanned all over and as he became aware of her scrutiny he turned away, saying:

'If you wish to swim, don't let me stop you. You will come to no harm here.'

Christina hesitated, her hands on her hips, unconsciously alluring in the white bikini. 'Aren't you going to swim?' she exclaimed.

'Not now.' Dom Carlos slid dark glasses on to his nose and sought the shade of the awning.

Christina pressed her lips together. 'Why?'

Dom Carlos bent his head. 'Miguel cannot be left alone.'

Christina stubbed her toe impatiently. 'He's asleep. He'll sleep for a while yet.'

He looked up at her then. 'You are eager for my company, *menina*?'

Christina thought he meant to disconcert her, to embarrass her as he had done before, but she would not allow him the satisfaction. At times like this she sensed she had a certain control of the situation. Now she said: 'You must be hot, too. Why won't you swim with me?'

His face stiffened, and he drew off the dark glasses. She saw his anger, and her heart pounded heavily. One day she would say too much and regardless of Miguel's needs he would dismiss her on the spot. 'Are you aware, Miss Ashley, that your appearance alone would be sufficient to scandalise most of my friends? Such attire may be commonplace on the beaches of Olhao and Faro and other holiday resorts of the world, but not here!'

Christina felt her cheeks burning. 'What is wrong with—with my attire?' she burst out hotly.

He slid the glasses back on to his nose. 'I would rather not enter into an argument with you, *menina*,' he replied infuriatingly.

Christina stepped to the side of the vessel and looked down into the water again. It was tantalisingly inviting, and she was hot, doubly so now since Dom Carlos's scathing remarks.

Without asking his permission, she climbed up and dived over the side, gasping as she hit the cold water.

It was warmer than British waters she had swum in, but nowhere near as warm as the shallows below the *quinta*.

Even so, after a few minutes she got used to it, and struck out strongly for the shore. She couldn't see Alfredo, but the beach looked inviting.

It was further than she had expected, and by the time she dragged herself out on to the beach, she was exhausted. She lay supine on the sand, digging her nails into the grains wearily.

At last she recovered sufficiently to look out to sea again, and propping herself up she focussed on the yacht. It seemed a terribly long way away, and she rolled on to her stomach impatiently, aware of an awful fluttering in her stomach when she recalled those last few moments before she dived over the side. Dom Carlos had made her feel small and cheap, and it was not a pleasant experience.

Dusting the sand off her already drying legs, she got to her feet and walked some little way up the beach towards the cliff face. Now she could see there were clefts in the rock and she wondered if there were caves beyond. It was likely. The whole area was honey-combed with fissures and crevices.

She peered into some of the crevices, but they were only cracks in the rock wall, big enough only for birds and sand crabs. She looked up and shaded her eyes against the glare of the sun. As Dom Carlos had said, the cliffs were impregnable, the upper half belling out above her and concealing the highest point. Anyone stranded here could hope for no escape except by sea.

Further along the beach at the point where the jagged formation of rock began its march into the ocean she found a cleft bigger than the others, big enough to slide between. Curiosity compelled her to penetrate its interior and to her surprise she found quite a large cavern. But it was not a pleasant place, it smelled strongly of dampness and stale seaweed, and she thought anyone would have to be hard put to spend more than a few minutes there. However, to her surprise she saw a pile of rotten boxes in one corner and she hesitated uncertainly before approaching them, wondering with an innate sense of the ridiculous whether she had inadvertently stumbled on someone's smuggling activities.

But further investigation, albeit of a timid nature, revealed nothing more than crumbling timbers and some grey powder which scattered on the ground at her feet when she touched it. It clung to her fingers and she rubbed her hands together vigorously to get rid of it.

There were more boxes at the back of the cave, but she didn't disturb them. Like the ones she had touched they were rotting and smelt strongly of decay.

With a sigh she turned back to the shaft of sunlight emanating through the crack in the rock wall. If she had not found the idea of being stranded on the beach appealing, she found the idea of being imprisoned in this rocky cell infinitely less inspiring, and she had the urgent desire to get out of the cloying dankness as quickly as possible.

She quickened her step, but as she reached the crevice and turned to slide through it a shadow darkened the shaft of sunlight and she stepped back a pace as a man's leg was thrust between the cleft almost touching hers. Shadowed by the brilliance outside, she could not make out who it was at once and certainly the man was blinded by the sudden dimness.

But he seemed to sense that someone was there, for he said: '*Meu Deus*, Christina, is that you?'

Christina went limp. 'Oh, it's you,' she breathed, recognising Dom Carlos's voice, but she was not prepared for the savage way his hands shot out and grasped her arms, dragging her forward almost ruthlessly. In the dim light he glared down into her startled eyes, his own glittering with anger.

'*Com e breca!*' he snapped harshly. 'What do you think you are doing? Have you not heard me calling your name?'

Christina shook her head helplessly, her wet hair falling in tendrils about her cheeks. Dom Carlos had shed his shorts to reveal swimming trunks, but he was still wearing the cotton shirt and it was soaked and clung to his muscular flesh.

'I—I'm sorry,' she began weakly. 'And no, I didn't hear you calling. I would have answered. I—I've been in this cave a few minutes—looking at those old boxes——' She turned her head in the direction of the back of the cave.

'The old arms dump, I know,' he muttered grimly. 'Hadn't you the sense to realise that you would be missed, that we would wonder where you had gone?'

Christina tried to take a step back. He was shaking her ever so gently and her bare leg had touched his and she couldn't bear that indifferent contact.

'You knew I had gone swimming,' she protested.

'But not this far,' he retorted. 'I imagined you would return to the yacht, not make for the shore. I have been half out of my mind with anxiety!'

Christina trembled. 'I shouldn't have thought my disappearance would cause you much concern,' she countered. 'I thought my—my appearance scandalised you!'

'You are mocking me,' he accused her fiercely, and his fingers tightened convulsively on her arms, drawing her closer to him, making her aware that he was trembling, too, his skin chilled and damp.

Christina looked up at him in the half light and her pulses raced alarmingly at the look in his eyes. She wrenched herself away from him then, not wanting to prolong the exquisite agony of being so near and yet so

143

far from him. 'Let's go outside,' she said unsteadily.

Dom Carlos put a tortured hand to his scarred cheek. 'Do I terrify you so?' he asked bitterly. 'Do not be alarmed. I won't—touch you!'

Christina hesitated a moment, looking back at him, and then she squeezed herself through the crack and out on to the sunlit beach. She took a deep breath of fresh air, shaken by the strength of her emotions. She had wanted him to touch her in that semi-darkness, she had wanted to feel his hands upon her, and the realisation was terrifying in its futility.

She turned as he pressed his body between the rocks and emerged into the sunlight, and saw with some anxiety that his face was pale beneath the tan. He was shivering and she forgot everything else in the concern of the moment.

'You're chilled to the bone!' she exclaimed, going close to him and staring up at him impatiently. 'What on earth have you got that wet shirt on for?'

Before he realised what she intended to do and could stop her Christina had loosened his shirt and reaching up had tugged it half way off his shoulders. He protested violently then, tearing the garment from her unresisting fingers, but it was too late. Christina had seen what it was he had wanted to conceal; why he had refused to remove his shirt himself.

Across his shoulder and down the side of his chest the skin was white and puckered, the marks of skin grafts evident against the darker flesh. The scars were much worse than the one on his face and because they were not being continually exposed to the elements they remained unhealthily pale.

'Oh, *Carlos!*'

Christina was scarcely aware that she had used his name. She just stood there looking at him, a terrible feeling of compassion welling up inside her.

His face contorted as he interpreted that look on her

face and his lips twisted. 'So now you know,' he ground out harshly. 'Not a pretty sight, is it?'

Christina didn't know what to say, what to do. She had never been confronted with such a situation and she felt herself to be hopelessly inadequate to cope with it.

'I—I didn't know,' she whispered huskily.

'No. How could you?' He moved to fasten his shirt again, but impulsively she reached out and stilled his hands.

'Don't,' she said. 'Don't keep it on. It—it's wet and you're frozen already. Take it off. *Please!*'

Carlos looked down at her hands gripping his arms, his jaw taut, a muscle jerking in his cheekbone. 'I would not wish to offend your eyes in such a manner,' he said savagely, and she looked up at him helplessly.

'It doesn't—offend me!' she denied heatedly. 'It was a shock, yes. How could it not be? But that's all. It's over now. I've seen it!'

Her eyes implored him to believe her and he bent his head, raising her hands to his lips in a suddenly disturbing gesture. Christina felt her breath quickening as she looked down on that raven dark head bent to her hands, and when he lifted his eyes and looked into hers she shivered, but not with cold.

'Thank you,' he said huskily, dropping her hands, and then with a stiffening of his shoulders he turned away.

Christina stared at the back of his head impotently. All of a sudden it had all been too much for her and she felt hot tears rising to the backs of her eyes. But he must not see her cry. He would misconstrue her motives. He would think she was crying out of pity, when in actual fact her reasons were much deeper, much more distressing from her point of view. She had heard friends, contemporaries, talk of love as something rather naïve, something one felt for a moment and then dismissed until it was necessary to feel it again. Some of her more experienced girl-friends had said it was always better to imagine oneself in love with the boy-friend of the moment, but as Christina had never had any serious affairs she had listened to their cynicism without rancour.

But suddenly she knew they were all wrong, terribly wrong. Love was not like that. It couldn't be turned off and on like a tap. It crept up unawares, and before one was conscious of it, one was trapped in its coils as surely as the fish in the net.

And that was what had happened to her, she was realising now. She had never been completely unaware of Dom Carlos, but in the beginning that awareness had been caused by antagonism. It was only as the weeks went by and she got to know him better that she had begun to be aware of him as a man; a man moreover whom it would be fatally easy to love.

And now she loved him, while he still regarded her as a rather annoying adolescent.

He was waving now to Alfredo Seguin on the deck of the *Turbilhao*, and presently she saw Alfredo toss the inflatable dinghy over the side and lower himself into it.

Carlos turned back to her, his face controlled again. 'Alfredo will take us back to the yacht,' he said formally. 'I am sure you would prefer that to swimming against the tide.'

Christina bent her head. 'Of course.' Her tone was subdued.

He studied her intently. 'Is something wrong?' he asked.

Christina looked up then. 'Apparently not,' she retorted, whipping up an anger she did not feel to hide her disturbed emotions. 'Is Miguel awake?'

'Perhaps. I don't know.' Carlos frowned. '*Menina——*'

'Oh, for goodness' sake, call me Christina!' she exclaimed. 'You called me that a few moments ago. Anything else would be futile now!'

His eyes narrowed. 'I have your permission?'

'Permission? Permission? What is that?' Christina moved past him unhappily. 'Must you always be so formal? Why are you afraid of behaving naturally? Today for the first time——'

'We will forget about today,' he said stiffly.

'Oh, will we? Are you commanding me, Dom Carlos?' Christina was past caring what he thought of her.

He clenched his fists. 'Christina——'

'Here's Alfredo!' Christina ignored his tormented exclamation, and leaving him she ran down the beach to greet the chauffeur with an assumed eagerness.

When they got back to the yacht Miguel was just waking up and Christina wondered however she was going to behave normally for the rest of the day. How could she encourage Miguel to enter the water, to share with him his little moments of achievement, under his uncle's eye? She wanted to get away from all of them, to be alone, to lick her wounds in private.

CHAPTER NINE

But in fact nothing was expected of her. Dom Carlos
suggested to Miguel that he might like to go ashore in
the dinghy with himself and Alfredo, and Miguel
agreed, eager to see a little of the marine life visible
beneath the clear waters of the cove. Dom Carlos did
not ask Christina if she wished to join them, although
his brooding gaze flickered over her as she put on her
skirt and blouse again, and she told herself she was
glad to be left alone aboard the yacht.

By the time they returned it was late afternoon and
Dom Carlos decided to head for home. Miguel seemed
contented after his excited day and chattered to Christina about what he had seen. Christina thought that
for once Dom Carlos had forgotten to be formal with
his nephew and Miguel had responded accordingly.

For Christina it had been a curiously exhausting
day. She had a pounding headache by the time they
had driven back to the *quinta*. She was glad to seek the
comparative sanctuary of her room, and she sent a
message down later with one of the maids that she
would not be joining Dom Carlos and his aunt for
dinner that evening.

During the next few days, Christina used Miguel's
reviving interest in himself to hide her own anxieties.
It was possible, by concentrating completely on what
she was doing, to shake off the terrible depression
which gripped her sometimes at the realisation that in
seven weeks she would be back at the university in
London.

Dom Carlos went about his estate duties as usual, sometimes joining Christina and his aunt for dinner, and at other times dining out. One evening, when her curiosity got the better of her, Christina said tentatively:

'Miguel told me that Dom Carlos was once engaged to a woman whose surname was Almeda. Are these the same Almedas he dines with sometimes?'

Donna Inez looked slightly taken aback. 'Miguel should not gossip,' she said severely, and then pushed aside her soup bowl. 'As a matter of fact, yes. The Almedas are old friends of the family.'

Christina concentrated on the wine in her glass. 'I see. And—and does Senhorita Almeda still live with her parents?'

Donna Inez frowned. 'You are a very inquisitive young woman, Miss Ashley. I do not see what business it is of yours.'

Christina managed to control her blushes. 'Perhaps not.' She looked up at the older woman squarely. 'I was just interested to know how a woman like that can live with herself.'

Donna Inez stared at her. 'I beg your pardon, Miss Ashley.'

Christina ran her finger round the rim of her glass almost absently. 'She did break the engagement after Dom Carlos's—accident, did she not?'

Donna Inez's eyes widened and then she shook her head impatiently. 'I honestly do not see what this has to do with you, Miss Ashley.'

Christina sighed. 'Of course it has nothing to do with me. As I say—I'm curious, that's all.'

Donna Inez wiped the corner of her mouth with her napkin. 'You make it sound as though Senhorita Almeda broke her betrothal with Carlos because of the accident,' she said disdainfully.

Christina's eyes narrowed. 'And didn't she?'

'Heavens, no!' Donna Inez stared at her with hauteur. 'It was nothing like that. Carlos and Sara had been betrothed for years. Since they were little more than children. It had become a habit. The fact that the rings were returned within weeks of the plane crash had nothing to do with it! Good heavens, they're still good friends!'

Christina took a deep breath. 'That is not what Miguel thinks,' she stated definitely.

Donna Inez's brows drew together. 'You are being melodramatic, Miss Ashley.' She snapped her fingers, summoning the maid to take their plates. 'I can assure you Miguel knows the facts as well as anyone.'

Christina rested her elbow on the table, cupping her chin on her hand. Outside the whirr of the night insects provided a constant background of sound, and a particularly persistent moth was trying to commit suicide against the globe of the lamp in the corner. It was all very remote and peaceful, but Christina was no longer at peace. She wished she dared ask Donna Inez more about the plane crash. She wished she dared question her about Dom Carlos's relationship with his nephew. She wished she could face Dom Carlos himself with Miguel's distorted beliefs.

But how could she do any of these things? Donna Inez did not like her. She was here on sufferance, that was all, and no doubt the older woman would take the greatest pleasure in informing Dom Carlos of Christina's inquisitive interest in his affairs. And as for asking Dom Carlos himself about his personal relationships ... She sighed. She could never get close enough to have that kind of conversation with him. Which only felt Miguel, and Miguel shied away from any discussion of the plane crash.

The following afternoon therefore she was surprised to be summoned to Dom Carlos's study. She went on reluctant feet, making sure the skirt of her apricot dress was uncreased and that her hair was subdued by an elastic fastener.

When she entered his study, Dom Carlos rose from his desk and indicated that she should be seated. Christina subsided into the chair with misgivings. She hadn't the faintest idea why he had sent for her, and she sought about in her mind for some possible reason.

Dom Carlos regarded her thoughtfully for a few moments and she took the opportunity to study him covertly. In a suit of beige silk, the narrow-fitting trousers accentuating the long muscular legs, he looked every inch the Portuguese nobleman, and remembering their encounter on the beach she could hardly credit her own temerity.

'My aunt tells me you have been asking about my relationship with the Almedas,' he said, shocking her into awareness.

Christina swallowed with difficulty. 'That's right.'

'Might I ask why?'

She looked furtively at him, wondering whether he was angry that she should have dared to show curiosity about his affairs.

'I—Miguel seems to believe your betrothal was broken as a result of—of——'

'As a direct result of my injuries?' he questioned curtly.

'Well—yes.'

'Why do you say this?'

'He told me.'

Dom Carlos smote his fist into the palm of his hand. 'Do you really expect me to believe that?'

'Why shouldn't you believe it? It's the truth!'

'The truth!' His tone was scathing now. 'Is it not perhaps truer to say that your curiosity got the better of you? That you could no more resist finding out the intimate details of my injuries than the moon can resist following the sun?'

'*No!*' Christina sprang to her feet. 'That's not true. If I'm curious about your affairs it's only on Miguel's account, nothing more.' But even as she said the words she knew they were not entirely true. She was curious about him, and she couldn't help it.

Dom Carlos's face was bleak and cold. 'What is it you want to know, Miss Ashley? Surely I should be the one to answer your queries?'

Christina clenched her fists. 'You make it sound horrible!' she cried.

'And isn't it? Wasn't it a horrible affair? Have you any idea how long Miguel and I lay in the ruins of the plane, the dead bodies of my sister and her husband beside us?'

Christina turned away. 'You're making it very difficult for me,' she protested faintly.

'But it's not difficult for me, of course?' he demanded fiercely, coming round the desk towards her. 'I am expected to discuss the intimate details of something that should have been forgotten long ago.'

Christina was conscious of him just behind her, and she hugged herself nervously. 'But it hasn't been forgotten, has it?' she asked. 'Miguel doesn't talk about it. You consider any enquiry to be an intrusion into your personal affairs. You constantly defend your appearance when no defence is necessary——'

'You think not?' he bit out violently, taking her by the shoulders and swinging her roughly round to face him. 'You think not?' His voice thickened. 'Could you bear to kiss me, Christina? Could you bear to press those soft cheeks against my face? Could you bear to wake in the morning beside someone who most closely resembles something out of a monster classic?'.

Christina struggled in his grasp, half afraid of his anger. She had never seen him so aroused, not even that day on the beach, and his hands were tightening, hurting her, digging into her shoulders like bands of steel. Then his face twisted, and he dragged her close against the hard length of his body, pressing his face—his scarred face—against hers.

Christina stopped resisting. The rough hardened edges of the scar bruised her cheek, but she didn't mind. It was ecstasy to be this close to him, to feel the heavy pounding of his heart beneath her fingers, to smell the clean male smell of him, and to know that for once she had broken down the barriers he had erected between himself and the rest of humanity. She felt his arms slide round her almost compulsively, and one hand tugged the securing band from her hair so that it fell thickly about her shoulders. His hands slid over her hips, moulding her body to his, and then his mouth moved across her face to hers.

Her lips parted involuntarily, and the kiss hardened passionately, demanding a response from her that she gave willingly. The warmth of her body seemed to go to his head and he burned her throat and neck with kisses, each one more urgent than the one before, so that a flame seemed to run through her, devouring any opposition she might have made to such brutally adult lovemaking. She had been kissed before, but never so intimately, never so expertly, never drowning in the drugging sensual emotions he aroused within her.

And then a shudder ran through him, and he uttered a groan of utter self-loathing, dragging himself away from her almost savagely, leaving her weak and swaying, completely bereft.

He raked a hand through his hair and said disgustedly: *'Deus*, I am sorry. I do not know what came over me!'

Christina cupped her neck with the palms of her hands, emotionally disturbed and unable to hide it. 'Oh, don't!' she cried, feeling actually physically sick now that he had let her go. How could he allow her to stay here after this?

'Christina! Christina, please!' His accent was thickening. 'I know my apology is inadequate, but what more can I say?' He looked at her searchingly. 'You have every right to be angry with me!'

'Angry?' Christina shook her head helplessly. 'Oh, God, Carlos, don't you know anything about women? Don't you know when saying you're sorry is not enough?' She put out a hand, unable to prevent herself, and touched the lapels of his coat.

But Dom Carlos turned abruptly away. 'I think it would be as well if we continued this conversation at some other time,' he said.

Christina's hand fell to her side. 'Of course,' she agreed tonelessly. 'You'll let me know when—when you want me.'

Dom Carlos made no reply, and did not turn, and with a shaking feeling inside of her Christina walked to the door. And for once he did not forestall her. She opened the door herself and went out quietly.

It was nearly a week before Christina saw Dom Carlos again. She knew he was avoiding her, and she told herself she ought to be relieved he had not found some reason to dismiss her, but it was useless to pretend that she didn't care. It was a painful agony preparing for dinner every evening not knowing whether she would find him at the table, and then a terrible anti-climax when again he was not there.

Thankfully Miguel noticed nothing amiss, and twice during that week Seguin took them driving so that Miguel might spend some time in the sea without Donna Inez and his uncle being aware of it.

However, on the evening of their second outing, Christina said: 'I really think you could use the pool now, Miguel. It's ridiculous pretending any longer. Your uncle and Donna Inez will have to know sooner or later.'

'No.' Miguel pursed his lips. 'No, I—they'd only feel sorry for me.'

Christina, her patience frayed by her own emotions, was unable to prevent herself saying: 'Why should they feel sorry for you? I should have thought the pity you feel for yourself was quite sufficient for one person!'

Miguel stared at her incredulously, and immediately she felt contrite. But it was no use attempting to take the words back now, they had been said, and she went on forcefully: 'It's true, Miguel! You actually told me you didn't want to walk again. I can't have sympathy for someone who takes such a defeatist attitude.'

Miguel's pale face was unusually flushed. 'I'm not a defeatist,' he denied hotly. 'And you don't understand.'

'Well, make me!' snapped Christina, staring at him, her hands on her hips.

Miguel hunched his shoulders. 'I can't.'

'Why not?'

'Because—well, because—I can't.'

'You mean you won't.'

'No, I don't mean that.' Miguel looked up at her unhappily. 'What would you do if you blamed yourself for someone else's unhappiness?'

Christina heaved a sigh. 'And whose unhappiness do you feel yourself responsible for? Your uncle's?'

Miguel bent his head. 'I didn't say I blamed myself for anyone's unhappiness,' he said moodily.

'No, but you do, don't you?' Christina shook her head. 'If you think your uncle's engagement was broken because of his injuries, you're mistaken! In any case, I can't quite see why you should blame yourself for the plane crash.'

Miguel stroked the polished wood arm of his chair. 'I don't want to talk about it any more.'

'Why not? Don't you think it's about time you did? I can't understand your reasoning. Your uncle's not an unhappy man—or at least if he is, no doubt his unhappiness is the realisation that you may never walk again.'

Miguel looked up. 'Why can't things go on the way they are? Why have you changed?'

Christina coloured now at his perception. 'Things haven't changed!' she exclaimed exasperatedly. 'It's just that—well—you've got to accept, Miguel, that in time everything alters. If for some obscure reason best known to yourself you imagine your uncle's life was ruined by this plane crash, don't you think you owe it to him to try and recover so that he can take up his life as it was before?'

'What do you mean?' Miguel stared at her.

Christina tugged abstractedly at a strand of hair, half wishing she had not started this conversation. 'Well, I mean—have you thought that your incapacity might be a barrier between him and a woman? That is—he might refuse to consider his own happiness while you are ...' Her voice trailed away. That aspect of the situation was difficult and she should not have brought it up.

'You mean—you mean you think some woman would marry him in spite of his scar?' Miguel looked astonished.

Christina felt angry suddenly. 'Of course they would!' she cried heatedly. 'Good heavens, Miguel, are you suggesting that because your uncle's face is scarred, that necessarily precludes any thought of marriage?'

Miguel looked uncomfortable. 'Well, nowadays people are so—so—and it's not just his face, you know.'

Christina was sick of the conversation herself now. 'Looks have very little to do with attraction, Miguel. You'll realise that as you get older. And you're deceiving yourself if you imagine the plane crash has had any disastrous effect on your uncle's affairs.'

Miguel shook his head. 'But you think, too, that I'm in his way.'

'I didn't say that.'

'No, but you meant it, didn't you?'

Christina's hands fell to her sides. 'Perhaps you should stop all this theorising and start acting. Go into the pool! Show your uncle you can move those muscles. With therapy I'm sure you could get out of that chair. I don't expect it will be easy; there'll be no miracle cure. But there's so much that can be done nowadays.'

Miguel looked into her face for a long moment and then sighed. 'What would you say if I told you my father was responsible for the crash?' he asked quietly, and Christina's attention was riveted.

'What are you talking about, Miguel?'

Miguel pressed his hands together. 'My father was responsible for the plane crash,' he repeated doggedly. 'He was! He took the controls when he had been drinking.'

'I see.' Christina frowned. 'This wasn't some scheduled flight then?'

'No. It was my uncle's plane. Tio Carlos was flying us—my parents and myself—to Marseilles. We were going on holiday. Then the crash occurred. It was terrible. My parents were killed instantly, but Tio Carlos and I survived. There was a fire . . .'

He broke off abruptly and covered his face with his hands. He did not cry; at least there was no outward sign of him doing so, but Christina felt his emotionalism.

She allowed him a few minutes, and then she said gently: 'But why haven't you discussed this with your uncle? Surely in the circumstances he was the one person to share your grief.'

Miguel dropped his hands and looked up, his face calmer. 'How could I?' he asked. 'In the beginning, my uncle was in hospital for a long time. He had to have many operations. His injuries were so much worse than mine, and he had been badly burned about the chest. When he at last came home, his betrothal to Sara Almeda was over, and he was scarred and bitter. I thought that was why; I thought he might be sorry that I was still here—to remind him of the crash, and everything.' Miguel looked very pathetic suddenly. 'As—as the days went by, it got harder, you see. My uncle didn't mention the crash to me, and I didn't know how to begin to talk about it. Can you understand?'

Christina nodded slowly. She was beginning to understand. She had had a taste of Dom Carlos's detachment herself, and she knew how days could build into weeks and weeks into months, with every added minute making the breaching of the gulf harder to achieve.

And three years ago, when the crash occurred, Miguel would have been only twelve years old. He would have had, indeed still had, no idea how to attempt to talk to his uncle, and because of his paralysis and the hopelessness of his condition, Dom Carlos had not known how to talk to him. They had both been victims of their own sensitivity, and because of this they had drifted further and further apart.

'But I still don't see why you've never wanted to walk again,' Christina persisted, knowing she had to get the whole truth out of him before he withdrew once more into himself.

Miguel's fingers closed round the arms of his chair tightly. 'I thought—I thought my uncle blamed me. For being my father's son.'

'Miguel!' Christina was shocked.

The boy sighed again. 'You don't understand why I felt that way. You see, Tio Carlos didn't want my father to take the controls of the plane. He knew he was not capable of doing so. Besides, although my mother was his sister, he did not—how would you say —get on with my father. But I didn't understand about my father, and I pleaded with my uncle to allow him to show what he could do . . .'

'Oh, Miguel! You weren't responsible for the crash,' Christina protested gently. But she could see the situation in the plane quite clearly. Dom Carlos, controlled as usual, flying the aircraft with the expertise he applied to everything he did; Teresa, his sister, Raoul, her husband, and Miguel; all passengers. She could even understand Miguel's pleas, his desire to prove that his father was every bit as capable as his uncle.

Miguel's lower lip trembled now. 'Perhaps not, directly,' he admitted jerkily. 'It was afterwards— afterwards I realised that I was the only one to suffer no permanent injury. My—my parents were dead. Tio Carlos was scarred for life. Only I had escaped.'

'But you were paralysed, Miguel!'

'I know. I know. But the doctors all said that I would eventually recover.'

Christina was beginning to see it all now. The apathy, the depression, the mental block; the desire to remain paralysed for good.

She got to her feet and stood looking down at him, an anxious expression on her face. 'And now?' she questioned. 'Can you see how futile your efforts have been?'

Miguel glanced up at her and then looked down again. 'You mean you think Tio Carlos wants me to walk again?'

'Of course he does.' Christina bent towards him. 'Miguel, you've got to understand that the things that are important to a boy are not necessarily important to a man. Your uncle has spent the last three years trying to find a cure for you. Do they sound like the actions of a man who doesn't wish to see you walking again?'

'N—no.' Miguel was tearful.

'There you are, then.' Christina heaved a deep sigh. 'Miguel, please believe me. You've got to stop pretending.'

Miguel nodded slowly, scrubbing the palms of his hands across his cheeks to hide the unmanly presence of tears. 'But don't tell Tio Carlos yet.'

'I must.' Christina shook her head. 'And tomorrow we'll use the pool again.'

Miguel looked hesitant. 'I—I will go in the pool. But please, don't tell my uncle. Just—just let him find out.'

Christina sighed. 'All right. All right, I'll agree to that. But you won't change your mind, will you? Promise?'

Miguel smiled faintly. 'Promise,' he said, and Christina felt suddenly weak with relief.

But lying in bed that night she had to accept what Miguel's recovery would mean to her. It didn't matter that it might be many months before he walked again; the breakthrough had been made and sooner or later he would respond to professional therapy. Once the idea was instilled in his mind that he should recover, the task was halfway done.

And so, in actual fact, she was redundant. She could even return to the hotel and spend the rest of the vacation with Bruce and Sheila.

The prospect filled her with dismay. She didn't want to leave the *quinta*. At least here she had the possibility of sometimes seeing Carlos. Back at the hotel it would be practically impossible.

Of course Carlos might decide to keep her at the *quinta* until the end of her holiday for Miguel's sake, but it was doubtful. And once Donna Inez knew what had happened she would do everything in her not inconsiderable power to get rid of Christina.

It was an agonising thought and Christina rolled on

to her stomach miserably. She thought how much easier her life would have been if she had just taken a job in London for the holidays and never come to Porto Cedro. She would never have bathed from Carlos's beach, she would never have met Miguel, and certainly she would not have found herself in love with a Portuguese nobleman who regarded her as a rather provocative adolescent...

CHAPTER TEN

THE following morning Christina awoke with a splitting headache. Her tongue felt dry and swollen, and although she got up and dressed she felt sick and miserable. When the maid arrived to place her usual tray of rolls and coffee on the balcony outside her room she looked aghast at Christina's appearance.

'*Ola, senhorita*, are you ill?'

Christina shook her head weakly. 'I don't know. I don't feel so good.'

'*Nao*, you look *terrivel, senhorita*.' The maid glanced round at the crumpled bed. 'You should not be up, *senhorita*.'

Christina thought of her conversation with Miguel the evening before. 'I'll be all right,' she insisted. 'I've probably got a chill or something.'

The maid regarded her doubtfully. 'The Donna Inez should be told,' she said at last.

'Heavens, no!' Christina shook her head, sitting down weakly at the glass-topped table and making a pretence of pouring herself some coffee when in actual fact the aroma of the continental liquid nauseated her. 'I'll take a couple of aspirins. I'll be fine.'

The maid departed, looking back uncertainly, and Christina pushed her chair away from the table and rising to her feet made her way back into her bedroom. She flung herself down on the bed, raising a hand to her eyes to shade them from the glare of the sunlight outside and thought how unfair life could be. Just when she was making real progress with Miguel this had to happen, and the thought of putting on her swimsuit and entering the pool sent shivers of chill down her spine. She knew she was running a temperature, she could feel the heat of her forehead penetrating to her fingers, and she drew a shaking breath wondering what was really the matter with her.

She must have fallen into an uneasy doze, and she was awakened by a sharp knocking at her door and a few moments later Donna Inez entered the room.

Christina sat up immediately, then gasped as a pain rent her temples at the sudden movement. She pressed her fingers to her head and said faintly: 'Good morning, *senhora*. Wh—what can I do for you?'

Donna Inez advanced to the bed without speaking and put out a hand and touched Christina's fiery skin. Then she glanced round at the maid who was hovering near the doorway and nodded briskly. When the maid had left them, Donna Inez clicked her tongue.

'You were surely not intending to associate with Miguel with a temperature such as you have!' she exclaimed shortly.

Christina heaved a sigh. She had not thought of that aspect of it. 'I—I thought it was a chill, nothing more, *senhora*.'

'Even so, it must have been obvious to you that you were in no fit state to attend to the boy. I have sent for Doctor Domingues. He will know what to do.'

'Oh, really——' Christina turned her head from side to side helplessly. 'It's not necessary. I'm just off colour, that's all.'

'Well! We shall see! I do not propose to take any chances where Miguel is concerned.'

Christina noticed with a trace of self-pity that at no time had Donna Inez expressed any anxiety on her account. She felt a choking feeling of desolation in her throat. No one really cared what happened to her. There was only Bruce—and he had Sheila, and she would always come between them. And here at the *quinta* she was completely alone. It was at a time like this that she realised just how alone she really was.

Donna Inez made her departure and Christina sank back against the pillows. She knew she ought to get out of bed and take off her clothes again, but she felt too weak. A wave of listlessness was sweeping over her and she just wanted to cry and cry . . .

Doctor Domingues was a charming man. He put Christina at her ease right away and after examining her pronounced that she had picked up a virus, probably on the beach. He said there was no cause for alarm, and that it was not contagious, but that she should remain in bed for the next few days and allow the antibiotics he was providing to do their work.

Christina protested that she would be perfectly all right once she had rested, but Doctor Domingues was adamant. And as Donna Inez stood at his elbow throughout the examination Christina knew that she would not be allowed to disobey the doctor's instructions.

To be truthful, Christina didn't remember much about the next twenty-four hours. The drugs Doctor Domingues had prescribed were a mild sedative and in her weakened condition she did little else than sleep, and she was amazed how limp she really was. Food was anathema to her and it was not forced upon her. She just drank and slept and gradually the enforced rest did its work.

In her more lucid moments she worried about Miguel, but in the beginning she was too weak to sustain such concern. She saw no one but Juana the housekeeper and the maid who brought her water to wash with and helped her to a drink when she asked for one. She hadn't seen Donna Inez again, and there was no one to tell her how Miguel was reacting to her illness.

But on the evening of the fourth day after she was

taken ill, when she was sitting by her open windows enjoying the scents from the blossoms which twined themselves round the pillars of the gallery, Donna Inez came to see her.

It was after dinner and Donna Inez was wearing the sleek black evening gown she had worn for the meal. Her hair was smooth and madonna-like, and Christina paused to wonder whether Donna Inez had not at any time found herself attracted to her nephew. After all, their relationship was not one of the blood. Donna Inez had married Carlos's uncle, and he had been a much older man. Christina had gleaned this knowledge from Miguel himself.

But now Donna Inez came across to her chair regally and looked down at her. '*Pois bem*, Miss Ashley. You are feeling better? Domingues tells me you are almost recovered.'

'Thank you, yes.' Christina managed a smile. 'He thinks I should be up and about again in two days.'

'So?' Donna Inez seated herself in the chair opposite. 'This is good news, is it not?'

Christina nodded. 'Oh, yes. I've—I've missed Miguel.'

Donna Inez frowned. 'Miguel? Oh, yes. Of course.' She pursed her lips as though reluctant to go on. 'He has asked for you, naturally.'

Christina relaxed. 'How is he?'

Donna Inez pleated the material of her skirt. 'There have been—developments, *senhorita*. While you have been ill.'

Christina frowned. 'Developments, *senhora*?'

'Yes, developments.' Donna Inez seemed to be finding it difficult to explain. 'With the assistance of Alfredo Seguin, Miguel has been into the pool.'

Christina's eyes widened. 'You mean—you mean—he actually went into the water?'

Donna Inez inclined her head. 'That is what I do

mean, yes.'

Christina felt a flood of excitement. 'Oh, but that's marvellous, isn't it? Does—does—his uncle know?'

'Dom Carlos is aware of what is going on, naturally, *senhorita*.'

The tone of Donna Inez's voice was chilling, and Christina found it difficult not to feel apprehension. 'And what did he say? What happened?' She was eager.

Donna Inez's nostrils flared. 'He was delighted, of course. It is only a pity that such a breakthrough should have been made at a time when you were incapacitated.'

Christina felt a sudden surge of anxiety. 'What do you mean?'

'Surely it is obvious, *senhorita*? Miguel has succeeded in making his first moves towards recovery without anyone's assistance.'

Christina was stunned. Was that really how they saw it? Was that how Miguel had *allowed* them to see it? When the moment of truth had come had he been afraid to tell them of those other occasions when he had hidden his efforts from them?

'I see,' Christina said now, faintly.

Donna Inez sighed with satisfaction. 'Naturally there is still a lot to be done. But Dom Carlos has contacted the physiotherapist in Lisbon already, and he is making arrangements to come to Porto Cedro to see Miguel for himself. One can only hope that the cure will be complete.'

'Yes.' Christina felt sick, but now it was not a wholly physical thing.

Donna Inez rose to her feet. 'I thought you would be pleased, *senhorita*. After all, you have been involved in Miguel's affairs as much as any of us recently. It is only a pity you were not there to see the culmination of all our hopes.'

'Yes.' Christina could think of nothing else to say.

'There are still several weeks of your holiday left, are there not, *senhorita*?' Donna Inez went on. 'Perhaps you would be glad of the opportunity to spend those weeks with your brother and his wife. After all, that is why you came to Porto Cedro, is it not?'

Christina nodded, terribly shocked and utterly bereft at the callousness of Donna Inez's dismissal. 'You mean—you would like me to leave, *senhora*,' she said slowly and distinctly.

Donna Inez had the grace to look disconcerted. 'I did not say that exactly, *senhorita*. But you must understand, your presence here at the *quinta* presents some problems now that Miguel is on the way to recovery. It is possible that Dom Carlos may be inviting some friends to stay, and the physiotherapist will be here to attend to Miguel . . .'

'It's all right.' Christina rose now, wrapping her gown closer about her. 'You don't have to make excuses to me, *senhora*. I understand perfectly. And besides, as you say, I have no function here now.'

'I'm glad you see it like that, *senhorita*.' Donna Inez smiled for the first time since entering Christina's bedroom. 'When shall I tell Dom Carlos you are leaving?'

Christina's stomach quivered. 'Would tomorrow be all right?'

'Tomorrow?' Donna Inez looked taken aback. 'I don't know about tomorrow, *senhorita*. I should have thought you would have wanted to spend a little time with Miguel . . .'

Christina stiffened her resolve. 'As Miguel seems to be getting along so well in my absence, perhaps it would be best to allow things to go on as they are. After all, my intervention for a short period only might upset him.'

Donna Inez frowned. 'You could be right, *senhorita*.

I will explain your views to Dom Carlos, and I am sure he will agree with them.' She walked towards the door. 'I must thank you anyway for being a companion to Miguel. I know he has enjoyed your stay enormously.'

The door closed silently behind her and Christina clenched her fists. She would have liked to have thrown something at that smugly closed door, but she quelled the childish impulse. Even so, she couldn't suppress a feeling of resentment, and she flung herself on her bed wearily, wishing for the umpteenth time that she had not been taken ill at such a crucial moment.

But as she lay there, she began to wonder whether she had not been a fool to accept Donna Inez's directions so obediently. After all, she knew Donna Inez had never liked her, had never wanted her in the *quinta*. She could quite easily be using Miguel's innocent venture into the pool as a lever to get rid of the girl.

Later, much later, she still lay awake, staring at the darkened ceiling, unable to relax, unable to accept the fact of her dismissal without an agonising sense of dread. Once Seguin drove her out of the gates of the *quinta* she would never come back, and once she had returned to the university she would never see Dom Carlos Martinho Duarte de Ramirez again.

Suddenly she heard voices on the patio below. They were subdued voices, but in her alert, wary state of consciousness she could hear every small sound.

She slid off the bed and padded to the french windows, peering out inquisitively. There were lanterns burning down on the patio, throwing shadowy patterns across the rippling waters of the pool. The musky scents of the flowers came to her nostrils, and she breathed deeply as the french doors blew gently wider.

But as she watched she saw a woman emerge from the shadow of the gallery and walk elegantly across the patio to gaze down into the pool, her dark hair silvering in the moonlight. She was a woman Christina had never seen before, small and slender, the weight of her hair almost seeming too much for the long pale neck. She was wearing a long evening gown of some soft drifting material that swirled about her ankles in the faint breeze.

Christina could not see her face, but she drew back nervously as Dom Carlos emerged from the shadows also to join her carrying two glasses, one of which he handed to the woman. She thanked him, the lilting sound of her voice holding a warmth that Christina sensed at once.

They were speaking together now, and Christina knew she ought to go back to bed. She was behaving like any common eavesdropper and she hated herself for being glued to the spot. They spoke in Portuguese so she could understand little of what was being said, but presently Carlos used the woman's name—Sara!

Christina drew her brows together. Of course, she should have guessed. This was Sara Almeda, the woman he had been going to marry, the woman to whom he had been betrothed since they were children.

Christina's interest quickened, but as she watched them she had to accept that everything Donna Inez had told her was true. Sara held no aversion for Dom Carlos's scarred face. On the contrary, from time to time she reached out a hand and touched him gently, and there was an easy cameraderie between them that had never borne the brunt of a misunderstanding.

Christina turned away abruptly. She had seen enough. She had no desire to hold the picture of them embracing in her mind for ever more.

She sought the silk covers of her bed, shedding her dressing gown and burying her face in the pillows. Tears that would not be denied pressed through her eyes and soaked the pillow beneath her hot face, but she scarcely noticed. She was lost in a world of utter despair. She no longer sought for reasons to stay at the *quinta*. She just wanted to get away, to escape, before she made a complete fool of herself.

The following morning, she was up and dressed before the maid brought her breakfast, and the servant stared at her in surprise when she saw her packed suitcases.

'You are leaving, *senhorita*?' she exclaimed.

'Yes.' Christina managed a smile. 'Would you ask Seguin to be ready about ten-thirty? I have to see Dom Carlos before I go, but ten-thirty should be all right.'

The maid shook her head. 'And what of the *menino*, *senhorita*? You will see him before you leave?'

Christina sighed. 'I—naturally.'

'*Sim, senhorita.*' The maid went away doubtfully, looking back with troubled eyes.

Christina poured herself some coffee and tried to relax. There was absolutely no reason for her to feel so tense. Doubtless Dom Carlos would be glad to see the back of her. He had shown by his avoidance that he could well do without seeing her.

However, when a knock came at her door a few moments later the very last person she expected to see was her employer. Hardly waiting for her summons, Dom Carlos strode into the room and Christina stared at him in astonishment.

Dom Carlos looked down bleakly at the packed suitcases and then fixed her with a hardening glare. 'Well, *menina*?' he snapped shortly. 'What is going on here?'

Christina heaved a sigh. 'Surely it's obvious, *senhor*. I'm—I'm leaving.'

Dom Carlos smote a hand to his forehead. 'I can see that that is your intention. What I demand to know is why?'

Christina spread a helpless hand. 'I was coming to

see you, *senhor.* I—how did you find out?'

'I overheard the servant telling Juana to send a message to Seguin that he would be needed later in the morning to drive the *senhorita* to the Hotel Inglês!' He took a deep breath and seemed to be attempting to compose himself. 'And now, please: what is going on?'

Christina poured herself more coffee with an annoyingly unsteady hand. 'Donna Inez told me that Miguel has been in the pool with Seguin and that he's agreed to your sending for the physiotherapist——'

'So?'

'So I'm not needed here. I mean—my sole purpose was to encourage Miguel to agree to treatment. Now that that's happened——'

'I employed you, *menina.* I will decide when you are to be dismissed.'

Christina forced herself to sip her coffee. Then she looked squarely at him. 'Are you going to try and force me to stay here against my will?'

'Must I do that? I thought you wanted to help Miguel——'

'I did. I *do.* Oh, what's the use? I can't pretend any more. I can't stay here—near *you* . . .' She turned away.

'*Por amor de Deus*, Christina, is this true?' he demanded in a tortured voice. 'I had no idea! I never dreamed——' His voice broke off and when he spoke again he was once more in control of himself. 'Naturally, if that is the way you feel, I will not stop you.'

Christina turned slowly. 'You—you understand?' she breathed incredulously.

'But of course,' he replied, and his tone was chilling. 'I will have your salary accounted and sent on to you.' He moved stiffly towards the door. 'And now—if you will excuse me . . .'

After he had gone Christina felt numb. She had felt bad before, but never like this. Despite everything that had gone before he was capable of allowing her to walk out of his life without so much as a tentative appeal to her to stay. She shook her head helplessly. She had been right to decide to go. There was nothing for her here.

Which only left the problem of Miguel ...

By the time she had tidied her room and carried her suitcases downstairs it was getting quite late and she knew Miguel would be having lessons with Senhor Perez. Deciding she could not possibly go without saying goodbye to him, she made her way to his apartments, and as on that other occasion she encountered Senhor Perez in the corridor. He stared at her in surprise, and said: 'Yes, *senhorita*? Can I help you?'

Christina looked beyond him to the door of Miguel's schoolroom. 'I'm leaving today,' she said. 'I've just come to say goodbye to Miguel.'

Senhor Perez frowned. 'I was aware of your departure, *senhorita*. Donna Inez told me last night that you would be leaving today.'

Christina managed a faint smile. 'Where is Miguel?'

Senhor Perez sighed. 'He is working, *senhorita*. And I feel I should tell you that Dom Carlos is of the opinion that your seeing Miguel before you leave is not a good idea.'

'Not a good idea?' echoed Christina. 'What do you mean?'

Senhor Perez held up his hand at her rising voice and indicated that they should move a few yards further down the corridor. 'Dom Carlos thinks that your sudden departure could be bad for the boy. At the moment, he still believes you are ill, confined to your rooms. Dom Carlos thinks it would be best if Miguel continued to think in this way, and then gradually, as your image fades, and other activities come to take its place. he will break the news that you have left.'

Christina's cheeks were paler than ever by the time Senhor Perez had finished. 'When did Dom Carlos tell

172

you this?' she questioned angrily.

'Just a few minutes ago, *senhorita*.'

Christina heaved a sigh. If Perez had said the night before she would have known he was lying. Carlos had not known himself that she was leaving until an hour ago.

'I see,' she said now. 'And of course, you agree with Dom Carlos?'

'Of course, *senhorita*. After all, what good can your seeing him do? It will only upset him unnecessarily. He has grown a great attachment for you, you must know.'

Christina thought that those last words were the sugar to sweeten the pill. But she had no fight left in her any more. After all, Carlos was right. It would be almost certain to upset Miguel when he found she was leaving, and maybe it would be better to give him more time to get used to being without her before breaking the news.

'All right,' she agreed with a shrug of her slim shoulders. She had lost weight during the last few days and the bones of her shoulders stuck through the thin material of her sweater.

'I am glad you see the truth of it,' Perez said, almost smugly, and Christina had a moment's desire to brush past him again as she had done before and go and see Miguel for herself.

But it was only a momentary thing. She was glad that Miguel had proved himself capable of acting on his own initiative and she would not risk that for anything.

She did not see Dom Carlos again before she left, but Donna Inez came to see her off. She shook hands politely and raised a hand in farewell as the sleek limousine moved majestically down the drive.

Christina lay back in her seat, dry-eyed and miserable. She had not wanted to come to the *quinta*, but it was twice as bad leaving it.

Bruce and Sheila accepted her return to the hotel almost indifferently. Obviously they had no idea of the emotional elements involved, and the fact that Miguel was at last beginning to make progress was sufficient to account for Christina's sudden appearance.

In a few days it was almost possible to view the weeks spent in the luxurious surroundings of the Quinta Ramirez as little more than a wild dream, and although Christina had a permanent ache in the region of her heart, there was no outward sign to indicate the precarious state of her emotions.

She took up her friendship with Julio and that young man was only too delighted to renew their acquaintance. They swam together, played tennis together, and once they all went out on Bruce's boat, Sheila included.

The weather was very hot and sultry, and Christina was tanned a deep brown. But she had not recovered her loss of weight and Maria was constantly ridiculing the small amount she ate, pressing food on to her in an effort to put flesh on her bones. Christina resisted, eating little, sometimes longing for her eventual return to London, and sometimes dreading such an inevitable step.

One afternoon when Bruce had planned to take Christina and Julio to a nearby cove to practise skin-diving, Sheila was taken ill with a migraine and Bruce could not leave the hotel. Christina was terribly disappointed, but she understood Bruce's dilemma.

Instead, she and Julio walked down to the harbour and spent the afternoon clearing out the cabin and swilling the decks. It was hot work, the sun hanging overhead like a golden ball, burning down on them.

Christina looked longingly at the fishing vessels making their way out of the harbour for a night's fishing, and then looked at Julio. 'I wish I was going with them!' she said, with a sigh. 'It would be marvellous to get away from land for a while—to feel the Atlantic breezes cooling our faces.'

Julio smiled. 'You should not say such things,' he reproved, wagging his finger at her. 'You know your brother would not approve.'

Christina sighed. 'I know.' She emptied her bucket of water over the side and stood watching the ripples it made. 'But I wish we could go out all the same. It's so hot! Couldn't we just take a trip around the bay? Half an hour, no more. That's all I'm asking!'

Julio straightened from his task of polishing the rail. He shaded his eyes and looked towards the horizon. 'It's going to be stormy,' he pronounced. 'Do you see those clouds gathering over there? That's a portent of rough weather.'

Christina wrinkled her nose at him 'Of course you would say that, wouldn't you? I mean—it sounds better to make that kind of an excuse, doesn't it?'

She was goading him and she knew it, but she was so depressed, and so sick of doing nothing about it.

Julio looked put out. 'I can assure you, Christina——'

'Oh, save your breath!' Christina swung across the gangplank and began walking along the jetty. In jeans and a tight sweater, her hair a curtain of gold silk about her shoulders, she attracted attention as the flame attracts the moth, but she was completely unaware of it. She was feeling utterly dejected.

Leaving the jetty, she joined the holidaymakers on the beach, stretched out on their rugs and lilos, soaking up the sunshine with complete abandon. She envied them their indifference. It seemed years since she had been like that. Was it really only weeks?

She found a spot and stretched out, too. shading her eyes with her arm. The sand was warm beneath her body, and she thought she would swim later.

A rumble of thunder brought the holidaymakers upright on their lilos, and there was a hasty gathering together of towels and transistor radios as the clouds which Julio had pointed out earlier to Christina rose higher on the skyline. Christina watched the hurried activity without interest. She didn't much care whether it rained or not.

But she got lazily to her feet and walked further along the beach until she came to the wall which divided this beach from Dom Carlos's. The public beach was almost deserted now and on impulse she slid through the cleft and emerged on to the beach beyond.

She lay back, resting against the rock wall, and looked across the stretch of sands to the lift which gave access to the *quinta*. How many times, she wondered, had she and Miguel used that lift? How many times had she swum from this beach where once she had been an interloper?

And was again, a small voice inside her taunted. She should not be here. She was only surprised that after her previous trespass Dom Carlos had not bothered to have the cleft sealed up.

The sky was lowering by the minute and pretty soon a few drops of rain spattered on her bare arms. She looked about her. There was nowhere to shelter here. She would be completely exposed to the elements and unless she wanted to risk getting soaked to the skin she should start back right away. But the idea of returning to the hotel did not appeal to her, and she sighed impatiently.

Then she looked again at the lift. She would be able to shelter there, in the shadow of the overhanging cable car, and certainly no one was likely to come down to the beach in this weather.

She ran quickly across the sand and reached the cliffs as the first flash of lightning rent the black clouds overhead. A few seconds later there was a terrific crash of thunder and Christina thrust herself through the cables to shelter below the cage.

She was only just in time. A few moments later the rain came down in torrents, and a wind appeared from nowhere, whipping up the sand into her face. She cowered in the back of the shelter, sitting down in a corner, legs drawn up, arms wrapped round them, and shivered a little. There was something rather terrifying about a semi-tropical storm and although she had seen many storms before, this was by far the worst.

She sighed again, hoping Bruce would not worry about her. Surely he would think she was sheltering somewhere until it was over. No one in their right mind would venture out in this.

The storm seemed to go on and on. Just when she thought it was abating slightly, it would return in full force, lashing against the cliff face, causing the waves on the shoreline to spray their spume several yards higher up the beach.

Christina was beginning to wish she had gone back to the hotel when she had the chance. It was getting dark and it wasn't only the storm that was darkening the sky. It was getting late and pretty soon Bruce would begin to have worries about her.

She ventured to the edge of the enclosure and looked up at the sky overhead. Vaguely she sensed a lightening, and the air was much cooler now, as though the rain had washed the sultriness away. Surely it would be over soon.

It was almost completely dark before the rain turned to an inconsequent drizzle and she ran swiftly back across the sands to the fissure in the rocks through which she had come. She was getting wet, but it was nothing compared to the downpour she had just experienced.

Along at the harbour there were lights and activity. She was surprised to see so many people about at this time of night, particularly as the storm could have been expected to send everybody to their homes.

But as she drew nearer the excited crowd she realised that this was no ordinary occasion. Something must have happened, maybe there had been a capsize among the fishing vessels which had gone out earlier. Maybe someone had been drowned.

She pushed through the people gathered round the small harbour, curious to know what had caused such excitement. It would be something to tell Bruce and Sheila when she got back. It might serve to distract Sheila's attention from her own lateness.

But suddenly she saw Bruce and Sheila. They were standing by the harbour wall with several men, and even from a distance Christina could see that Sheila was upset. She was dabbing her eyes with a handkerchief and Bruce was comforting her.

But it was to the man standing beside Bruce that Christina's eyes were drawn. A tall, lean, dark man, whose cream pants and rough navy sweater were stained with seawater and whose usually immaculate hair was tousled and windswept as though he had been continually rumpling it with his hands.

A feeling of anxiety swept over Christina. What was Carlos doing here? There must have been an accident. But to whom? Miguel, perhaps?

Her heart rising into her throat, she pushed swiftly through the fishermen that stood between her and the group by the harbour wall, but as she did so, she became aware of an uncanny silence descending on the community.

Her brother and Sheila and Carlos Ramirez were attracted by the sudden stillness, and they turned and saw her almost simultaneously. Christina halted uncertainly, conscious of a look of incredulity spreading over their faces, and then to her astonishment, Carlos strode forward and grasped her shoulders, staring at her as though he couldn't believe his eyes. He muttered something under his breath in his own language which she felt sure was not complimentary, and then he said savagely:

'*Meu Deus*, Christina, where have you been? Don't you realise—we thought you had been drowned——'

He broke off to shake her impatiently and her hair fell forward across her eyes in strands of damp gold.

Bruce joined them, apparently seeing nothing strange in Carlos's concern. 'Come on, Chris,' he exclaimed. 'Did you take *Fantasma* out?'

Christina could hear Sheila sobbing openly now and uttering recriminations against her for being an irresponsible girl, and she tried desperately to gather her scattered wits.

'I—I'm sorry——' she began, her eyes wide and concerned. 'Please believe me, I'm sorry——'

Carlos's hands slid up her shoulders to cup her neck. 'But where have you been?' he demanded, and she paused to notice that his face was pale beneath his tan and that he seemed to care little for the fact that they had an audience of perhaps thirty or forty people, all of whom would find his reactions to the disappearance of the English hotel owner's sister rather startling. 'Are you all right? You're not hurt?'

'I—I'm fine,' Christina quivered, looking up at him tremulously, scarcely aware of Bruce and Sheila in that moment.

'Thank God for that!' muttered Carlos fervently, and then he ran a hand down his scarred cheek almost shakenly. 'Come! We cannot talk here. My car is parked over there——'

Bruce took Sheila's arm and they all walked across to where the sleek convertible was waiting. There was a murmur of speculation from the crowd and Bruce shrugged his shoulders helplessly at Sheila as she made a bewildered gesture.

Christina was too bemused to know half of what was going on, but she turned to Bruce, saying helplessly: 'What is all this? Why did you think I might be drowned? That I might have taken *Fantasma* out?'

Carlos put her into the front seat of the car without allowing her any opportunity to protest. 'Your brother's boat was found splintered on the rocks some distance down the coast,' he said distinctly.

Christina's lips parted and she gazed up at Bruce. 'But how——?'

'That's what we'd all like to know,' snapped Sheila, drying her eyes.

'No doubt we shall in time,' observed Carlos coolly, 'Please to get into the car, *senhora*.'

Sheila had no choice but to do as he had directed and Bruce got in beside her while Carlos slid behind the wheel. The crowds were dispersing as the convertible moved sleekly up the road to the village and Christina glanced round at her brother and his wife almost shamefacedly.

'I—I was sheltering,' she explained awkwardly. 'That was all. Sheltering!'

She heard Carlos utter a derisive ejaculation, but whether it was directed towards her or himself she could not be certain.

They reached the road where the hotel was situated and the three passengers were taken aback when Carlos turned pointedly in the opposite direction.

'We will go to the *quinta*,' Carlos said, by way of an explanation. 'There are things to be said which are better said there, I think.'

Bruce looked bewilderedly at his wife and Sheila drew down the corners of her mouth sulkily. In her opinion far too much fuss had been made already over Christina's disappearance and so far as she was concerned what the younger girl needed was discipline not sympathy.

Even so, both Bruce and Sheila were charmed by the appearance of the *quinta*, and when they entered the magnificence of the arched hall they could not help but be impressed.

Carlos took charge of everything. Christina found the whole affair too confusing to be speculated upon and there were so many questions she wanted to ask and couldn't.

Donna Inez came into the hall at their entrance and viewed her nephew's appearance with obvious distaste. 'You took out the yacht then?' she queried coldly, with scarcely a glance at his companions. 'You are a fool, Carlos!'

Carlos's jaw tightened and Christina drew in her breath sharply. What was going on? 'Perhaps so,' Carlos said now, non-committally. 'Will you go through?'

He indicated the small lounge to the right of the hall and Bruce took Sheila's arm to escort her into the room. But when Christina would have gone with them, Carlos stayed her with a hand on her arm, and she looked up at him perplexedly.

'Come,' he said. 'I wish to speak with you.'

Donna Inez twisted her lips. 'You are a fool, Carlos!' she repeated furiously. 'You cannot seriously be contemplating such action!'

Carlos drew himself up to his full height and even in the stained casual clothes he had the breeding and presence of his forebears. 'You will say nothing more, Inez,' he stated bleakly. 'And you will go with Senhor Ashley and his wife and offer them our hospitality. Some black coffee, perhaps, would not come amiss. Or something stronger.'

Donna Inez clenched her hands. 'You cannot do this to me, Carlos,' she exclaimed, and there was emotionalism in her voice.

'Please, Inez. Do you not think *you* have done enough?'

Inez looked as though he had struck her, but then, like Carlos, she assumed her dignity. 'Very well,' she said tonelessly. 'But I shall be leaving.'

Carlos shook his head. 'I cannot make you stay.'

Christina had been conscious of Carlos's hand on her arm all the time he was talking to Donna Inez, and she sensed that Donna Inez was aware of it, too. But what did it mean?

Carlos released her then, and strode ahead of her down the corridor leading to his study. She followed him with reluctance, and when the door was closed he said: 'I am sure your brother will not approve of my actions, but for the moment I am prepared to risk his wrath. I must speak with you—alone.'

Christina trembled. 'Oh, yes?'

'Yes.' He stared at her for a long moment and she moved awkwardly beneath his gaze.

'Look,' she said unhappily, 'I know you've been worried—that you've all been worried, and I'm sorry, truly I am. But I never dreamt . . .' She sighed. 'I was sheltering below the *quinta.* In the lift shaft.'

Carlos smote a hand to his forehead. 'In the lift shaft! *Deus*, Christina, you have no idea of the anxiety you have caused me—in fact, all of us.'

'I know. But I couldn't help it. It—it was raining so hard and I was trapped until it stopped. I thought Bruce might be worried, but I never thought you——' She broke off abruptly and bit her lip.

'No,' he said heavily, walking across to his desk and leaning on it momentarily. 'No, you never thought I should find out and be concerned.'

'No.' Christina made a helpless gesture. 'How could I think that? So far as I was aware no one knew of my disappearance.'

Carlos straightened, his face grim. 'Nevertheless, I did know, and I was—worried.' His nostrils flared slightly. 'You heard Inez ask whether I had taken out the yacht; she was enquiring because when I found you were missing that is what I had to do.'

'And—and Bruce told you—the *Fantasma* was missing, too?'

'Of course.' Carlos drew a deep breath. 'In the circumstances, I was, as Inez has already said, a fool!'

Christina moved restlessly. 'But why did Bruce contact you? Surely he didn't imagine I was at the *quinta*?'

'Bruce did not contact me, Christina. I contacted him.'

Christina was puzzled. 'But why?'

Carlos heaved a sigh. 'I wanted to see you.'

'Why?' she repeated.

Carlos shrugged his broad shoulders. 'I wanted to put a proposition to you.'

'What kind of a proposition?'

'I wanted to ask you to return to the *quinta*. On a permanent basis.'

'What?' Christina was astounded. 'But how could I? The—the university——'

'Ah, yes, the university!' Carlos's lips twisted. 'You would have refused, no doubt.'

'What do you mean? I *would have*? Are you no longer intent on making such a proposition?'

'No.' Carlos ran a hand down his scarred cheek. 'No, I realise such a proposition would not be acceptable to you.'

Christina felt herself to be in a permanent state of tension. 'But why?' she exclaimed. 'Why should you want me back here on a permanent basis?'

A muscle jerked in Carlos's cheek, the only outward sign of his own tension. 'Why indeed?' he muttered, a trifle bitterly.

Christina took a shaking breath. 'Please,' she said, in an unsteady tone. 'Please, Carlos, explain to me——'

Whether her unconscious use of his Christian name

aroused him, or whether the tension of the search had been finally too much, Christina did not know, but when he turned and reached for her she did not resist.

'You will hate me for this,' he muttered against her mouth, 'but I must touch you once more. *Tu amo*, Christina *minha, tu adoro!*'

Christina understood enough Portuguese to know what he was saying, but she could hardly believe it. She thought he was carried away by his emotions, and it was enough for the moment just to cling to him, to slide her arms around his waist and press herself closer against the hard length of him. The possession in his hungry mouth destroyed her inhibitions, destroyed the carefully built-up façade of indifference she had meant to display. She was unwilling to move, unwilling to re-erect the barriers that were between them.

But finally he put her away from him, holding her at arm's length, staring at her with tortured eyes. 'What are you trying to do to me, Christina?' he demanded thickly. 'Don't you know what lovemaking like this does to a man? Are you such a child that you cannot see the danger?'

Christina shook her head. 'I'm not a child, Carlos. I never was.'

'Then why do you do this?' His fingers tightened on her shoulders painfully. 'Does it give you some strange thrill to torment me so?'

'I? Torment you?' Christina tried to struggle free of him, but he would not let her go.

'You have tormented me for many weeks, *amada*,' he muttered, huskily. 'And even now, even while my senses are inflamed by the way you responded to my kiss, I know that what I need of you you cannot give.'

Christina looked into his eyes. 'Carlos, what are you saying?'

He sighed. 'You are so young, Christina. You have your whole life in front of you, and to ask you to give

184

up your university training and live here at the *quinta* would be very wrong of me.'

'But, Carlos,' she began, but he put his fingers on her lips, stilling her protest.

'Please, let me finish,' he said. 'I realise this, and that is why you must forgive me if I have frightened you——'

'But you haven't frightened me!' Christina said fiercely. 'Carlos, please, what is it you want of me? A companion for Miguel? Or something else?'

Carlos's eyes were narrowed and she could not see their expression, only the smouldering glint from their tawny depths. '*Deus*, Christina, you ask *that* of me!'

Christina moved her head from side to side slowly. 'Then ask me! Tell me what it is you want of me!'

Carlos released her abruptly. 'You would have me grovel?' he asked, in clipped tones. 'You think I would not do it if I thought it would make any difference?' He turned away.

Christina looked at the back of his head lovingly, unable to deny any longer the surge of warmth that was rising inside her. Without stopping to consider the consequences of her action, she moved towards him, sliding her arms round his waist from behind, pressing her face against his broad back.

'If it's me you want, for myself,' she whispered. 'Then I'll stay—willingly.'

He turned, staring down into her upturned face. 'What are you saying? Is this some kind of joke?' he demanded.

'Does it sound like a joke?' she asked chokingly.

He shook his head slowly. 'But when you left you said you could not stay near me! Oh, please, Christina, do not allow the heat of this moment make you say things you do not mean! Believe me, if once I take you at your word, I will never let you go!'

Christina swallowed. Her throat was dry and she

could hardly think coherently. 'But you let me go!' she protested.

'Of course. I was stunned. I could not believe that you would walk out on me like that.'

'But Donna Inez——'

His brow darkened. 'Donna Inez? She has something to do with this? With your leaving?'

Christina put a hand to her forehead. 'I—I—perhaps not.'

'Tell me!' He was arrogant now.

'She—she told me that Miguel was recovering and that my services would no longer be needed——'

'But it was you who persuaded Miguel to try again,' exclaimed Carlos angrily. 'I naturally thought you would want to stay and see the culmination of our hopes——'

'I did.'

'And Inez said you should go.' Carlos's voice was hard as he said the words.

Christina was confused. 'Please—maybe I was too willing to believe her,' she began, unwilling to hurt the other woman.

'But did she not tell you how delighted I was? How Miguel had told us of your previous efforts with him?'

'No.' On this, Christina had no doubts.

'But naturally, Miguel told me. He was eager to do so. He was sorry you were not there, of course, but afterwards I think he was trying to make much progress so that he could astound you with his prowess.'

Christina half smiled. That sounded more like the Miguel she knew.

Now Carlos shook his head. 'And you let Inez send you away! And yet when I came to see you you told me it was because of me!' His fingers sought the disfiguring line on his cheek. 'Why? Was it—as I suspected—because of this?'

186

Christina was horrified. 'No. Don't even think such a thing.'

'Then why?' Carlos was impatient now to know the truth.

'The—the night before I left, I saw you and—and Sara Almeda in the patio.'

Carlos frowned. 'Yes?'

'Yes.' Christina spread her hands. 'Oh, Carlos, try to understand. I was in love with you, and I already knew I would have to leave. When—when I saw you two together, I couldn't bear it any longer.'

'And that is why—you said what you did?' He was incredulous.

'Oh, yes. Yes!'

Carlos bent his head, drawing her closer to him, burying his face in her hair. 'You love me!' he mouthed huskily. 'Oh, Christina, I adore you, and you have no need to fear Sara. The evening you saw us together she had come to the *quinta* to dine with Inez and myself and to see Miguel. She was leaving Portugal for some time to stay with friends in Canada, and she wanted to see the boy before she left.'

'Is that true?' Christina looked up at him.

'Of course it is true, *amada*. I would not lie to you.' Then he sighed. 'But Inez tried to make things difficult for us—for Sara and myself. You see, she had never completely given up hope that one day we might marry after all, and when Sara came to the *quinta* that evening, she made certain innuendoes which could not be misconstrued. It was most embarrassing, and that is why Inez is so unhappy now.'

'Does—does she know about me?'

Carlos smiled. 'Oh, yes, I am afraid she does, *amada*. I should not think anyone in Porto Cedro was left in any doubt of my feelings for you when I found you were missing this evening. Your brother knows, I am sure, but as yet nothing has been said.' He stroked her neck sending shivers of delight down her spine. 'He will probably object to me. I am too old for you.'

'You're not.' Christina reached up and touched her mouth to the corner of his.

'Oh, yes, I am, but I fear I do not care any more. I love you more than life itself, and to imagine letting you go now for whatever reason would kill me.' He shook his head a trifle bemusedly. 'I knew when I brought you to the *quinta* to be a companion for Miguel that I would not be able to let you go.' He smiled again. 'My water nymph,' he murmured.

Christina quivered. 'You were so angry that evening you found me swimming from your beach.'

Carlos nodded. 'I suppose subconsciously I resented the fact that your face enchanted me, that your youth reached out to me when I was scarred and old and ugly——'

'Never that,' murmured Christina softly. 'Oh, darling, what will Miguel think, do you suppose?'

Carlos chuckled. 'He will envy me. Perhaps he will even be a little jealous.'

Christina laughed. 'Oh, Carlos, I'm so happy!'

'But first we must go and tell your brother what he must do,' said Carlos firmly. 'And reassure him that he will have another boat. The *Fantasma* must have been swept away by the storm.' He smiled. 'I personally will provide him with a new one. But first there is a marriage to arrange.'

Christina's eyes twinkled. 'Oh, are we getting married?' she teased. 'I don't remember being asked.'

Carlos pulled her closely into his arms. 'But yes, there will be a marriage, *amada*,' he said, rather disturbingly. 'I do not intend our relationship to last for anything less than life ...'

❊ FREE ❊
*Harlequin Reader Service Catalog**

A complete listing of all titles currently available in
Harlequin Romance, Harlequin Presents,
Classic Library and Superromance.

**Special offers
and exciting
new books, too!**

*Catalog varies each month.

**Complete and mail
this coupon today!**

Take these 4 best-selling novels FREE

Take these 4 best-selling novels FREE

Yes! Four sophisticated, contemporary love stories by four world-famous authors of romance FREE, as your introduction to the Harlequin Presents subscription plan. Thrill to **Anne Mather**'s passionate story BORN OUT OF LOVE, set in the Caribbean.... Travel to darkest Africa in **Violet Winspear**'s TIME OF THE TEMPTRESS....Let **Charlotte Lamb** take you to the fascinating world of London's Fleet Street in MAN'S WORLD ....Discover beautiful Greece in **Sally Wentworth**'s moving romance SAY HELLO TO YESTERDAY.

Harlequin Presents...

The very finest in romance fiction

Join the millions of avid Harlequin readers all over the world who delight in the magic of a really exciting novel. EIGHT great NEW titles published EACH MONTH! Each month you will get to know exciting, interesting, true-to-life people . . . . You'll be swept to distant lands you've dreamed of visiting . . . . Intrigue, adventure, romance, and the destiny of many lives will thrill you through each Harlequin Presents novel.

Get all the latest books before they're sold out!

As a Harlequin subscriber you actually receive your personal copies of the latest Presents novels immediately after they come off the press, so you're sure of getting all 8 each month.

Cancel your subscription whenever you wish!

You don't have to buy any minimum number of books. Whenever you decide to stop your subscription just let us know and we'll cancel all further shipments.